THE SEVEN SLEEPERS SERIES

THE SWORD
of
CAMELOT

GILBERT MORRIS

MOODY PRESS

CHICAGO

© 1995 by
GILBERT L. MORRIS

ISBN: 0-8024-3683-8

10

Printed in the United States of America

To Staci and Kelli—
my beautiful granddaughters

Contents

1

A Long Journey to Make

Darkness had almost overtaken the small band emerging from the damp forest. For an hour now a steady rain had fallen, and all seven young people who trudged down the muddy road were soaked to the skin.

A lightning bolt scratched the darkness, blinding Josh Adams. Instinctively he twisted his head away and squeezed his eyes shut, then promptly stepped into a hole and fell sprawling.

"Josh—are you all right?" Sarah Collingwood was at his side in an instant, pulling at his arm. Unlike Josh, who was tall and gangly, she was small and graceful.

"The lightning didn't hit you, did it?" she asked in a frightened voice.

"No, it didn't—and you can let go of my arm. I don't need any help!"

Josh, at fourteen, was the same age as Sarah. However, he was the leader of this party, and it looked bad for the leader to fall flat on his face, so he pushed Sarah away almost angrily. He was easily embarrassed and already felt himself to be clumsy and plain. He scraped at the mud on his shirt in disgust. *Some leader I am—can't even stay on my feet!*

Then he glanced at the girl and noticed the hurt on her face. "I'm sorry, Sarah. I—I guess I'm a little bit on edge."

"I guess we all are," another voice said. Bob Lee Jackson paused beside him. Jackson was never known as anything but "Reb," for he came from the South. Another fourteen-year-old, Reb had light blue eyes and pale, sun-bleached hair.

"Do you have any idea where we are, Josh?"

"No, I don't," Josh snapped.

The others had caught up and now stood in a half circle, silently watching him.

"Well, don't look at me! It wasn't *my* idea to travel in this storm!"

This was the sort of thing Josh despised. Others in the group, he felt, were more capable leaders—people such as Dave Cooper. But it was he who had been chosen by Goel to head the party, so now he peered forward and shook his head glumly. "We'll just have to go on."

"We might not find a place to camp all night. Why don't we at least try to get under some trees?" Jake Garfield was a small boy of thirteen, and he looked thoroughly miserable. Water ran down his soft, black cap and dripped onto his shoulders. He shivered. "Looks like we'll have to wait till morning to find a place to stay."

"No, there's got to be something not too far. We can't stay out in this." Josh wheeled and marched off down the road, his feet squishing in the mud.

He had not gone more than a hundred yards when another lightning bolt rent the sky, this time not as brilliant. He batted his eyes and cried out, "Look up there—a house!"

Quickly the others moved forward. Dark as it was, a house of sorts could be seen nestled off the road under some huge elms. "That must be the house Goel marked on the map!" Josh cried excitedly.

"It looks like something out of an old TV series," Dave Cooper said grumpily.

Sarah agreed, and the others looked troubled by the appearance of the building before them. It was a small, forlorn-looking dwelling. But despite its gloomy appearance, Josh realized they had little choice.

"Come on," he said, ignoring their remarks. "At least it's got a roof and four walls. Goel said that they'd take us in—*if* it's the right place."

The seven sloshed up to the house, and—wiping the rain from his eyes—Josh knocked on the door.

It opened almost instantly, and the crackling in a large fireplace sent forth a cheerful sound.

"Who be you?" The speaker was a short, muscular man with a set of suspicious dark eyes. "What do you want?"

"We need a place to stay." Josh was aware of the quiver in his voice. "Go—"

"This ain't no inn. You'll have to go someplace else."

But before the man could slam the door shut, Sarah called out, "Goel sent us. He said you'd take us in."

"Goel? Well—that's different." He stared at them for a moment, then shrugged and stepped aside. "You'd better come in out of the wet." He called out, "Matilda, we have guests, guests from Goel."

Eagerly the young people entered the room and stood making puddles on the floor.

That seemed not to trouble their host, however. He said, "You'd better get out of them wet clothes." He peered at them once again and asked, "You say it was Goel who sent you?"

"Yes," Josh said eagerly. "He told us to wait here— that he'd come to us at your house. You *are* Crinen, aren't you?"

"Aye, I be Crinen." He turned away. "Matilda, take these girls to their room, and I'll take these young fellows to the attic."

The woman with merry blue eyes led Sarah and Abigail to a small room attached to the back of the house. "It ain't much," she said, "but at least you can get out of them wet clothes, and I'll fix you something to eat."

"Oh, thank you!" Sarah said warmly, and as soon as the woman left she began unpacking her knapsack. "It's a good thing we wrapped our clothes in oilcloth or we wouldn't have anything dry to put on."

"Well, I don't have anything fit to wear anyway." Abigail Roberts was a year younger than Sarah and much prettier—at least some thought so. She had blue eyes, blonde hair, and a small, graceful figure. Now, as she looked at the garment that had been wrapped in the oilcloth, she frowned in disgust. "This is the ugliest dress I have ever seen."

"At least it's dry."

Sarah put on her own dress, one much like Abigail's, and the two of them picked up their wet clothes. "Let's go by the fire. I hope they have something good to eat."

* * *

Crinen led Josh and the other boys up a ladder into the attic. The boy quickly saw that it was a neat room with a ceiling that sloped to a peak. There were only two beds.

Reb said, "Looks like some of us will have to bunk on the floor." "Oh, we've got plenty of bedding," Crinen said. "You can strip them clothes off, and I'll go see if Matilda has something for you to eat."

As soon as Crinen had disappeared, the boys began eagerly changing their clothes.

"I don't know how we're ever going to get these dry," Jake complained, wringing out his shirt. He watched it drip on the floor. "Maybe we can take turns putting them in front of the fireplace."

The smallest member of the group—Wash—was a black boy of twelve. He moved quickly and soon had on dry clothing. Then he stood watching the others. Glancing toward the opening that led from the loft, he said, "I hope they've got something to eat. My stomach feels like my throat's been cut!"

"Mine too," Reb said. He looked over at Josh. "How long you think we'll have to stay here?"

Josh was pulling a warm brown sweater over his head. "I don't know. Goel didn't say. But I hope it won't be too long, because it's going to be pretty crowded in here."

"Well now, let's go down and see if Miss Matilda has cooked up some vittles." Reb grinned and led the way down the ladder.

Everybody gathered in front of the huge fireplace. Soon the two girls joined them, and they stood greedily soaking up the heat.

Thirty minutes later they were seated at a large, wooden table, wolfing down steaming bowls of what appeared to be beef stew.

"This is *good,* ma'am!" Reb exclaimed. "I don't guess you got any grits to go with it—or hog jowl?"

Matilda paused from her task of stirring the stew and refilling Josh's bowl. "Grits? Hog jowl? No, we don't have any of that. This is just deer stew."

"Well, it's good, whatever it is," Josh said. "And being here sure beats sleeping out in the mud, doesn't it?" He devoured his stew eagerly.

Soon all of them were pleasantly satisfied. Then they sat around the fire, and its warmth began to make Josh, at least, very sleepy.

Crinen came to look at them. He cocked his head to one side. "Would you be telling me where you come from?"

11

Josh opened his mouth to answer. Then a thought came to him, and he closed it.

Sarah must have guessed what was on his mind. "Well," she said, carefully, "if you mean where we *just* came from, that would be the Kingdom of Atlantis."

Crinen stared. "Why, that's under the ocean! You couldn't live in a place like that! Only mermen and merwomen live there."

Sarah shook her head. "I'm afraid you're mistaken about that. Goel sent us there to do something for him. And now that it's done, he told us to come here."

Crinen looked at them incredulously. He scratched his head. "People living under the sea! If that don't beat all! And now ye be going somewhere else."

"Yes," Sarah said. She started telling him that they were not really from his world—that all seven of them were aliens and strangers.

She tried to put together the story of how nuclear war had come to the earth. "We were all put in time capsules —sleeping chambers—where we stayed in a suspended state for years and years." Then she related how they had been awakened and commissioned by Goel to do his bidding, which meant to combat the dark forces that were now sweeping over Nuworld.

Sarah realized that was too much to explain to Crinen, and she ended by saying simply, "We are the servants of Goel, and we go where he sends us."

Crinen's eyes brightened. "And that's what I be! Me and Matilda." Then a shadow crossed his face, and he lowered his head. "There be not many of us now. The Sanhedrin, they came here last month looking for someone. I don't trust those priests and this Dark Lord they talk about!" He shook his head violently. "I'll have nothing to do with him!"

"That's wise," Josh said. "The Dark Lord is an evil force, and Goel is the only hope for this world."

They talked for a while, but soon all heads were nodding. Josh snapped out of a doze long enough to say, "Let's get to bed. Goel may come early tomorrow."

The girls went to their room at once.

Josh and the boys talked a little more before going to sleep. The last thing Josh remembered was Reb saying, "I shore do wish Goel would hurry up! I purely do *hate* not knowing where I'm going or when I'm going to do something!"

* * *

Reb was due to be disappointed, for Goel did not come the next day—or the next week either.

The Seven Sleepers were glad to rest for a few days. Their journey from Atlantis had been difficult. However, as the week passed, they became edgy. There was nothing to do but walk through the woods, and the weather was turning colder.

Every night they would meet in the attic room before bedtime and talk of making plans, but there were no plans to be made.

"I don't like it," Reb complained one evening. He had been growing more and more impatient. Night after night he had expressed a desire to get on with it. "I want to be doing something!"

Dave Cooper's mouth turned down in a frown. "I'm tired of listening to you, Reb," he said shortly, "All you do is complain."

Ordinarily Reb would have turned off such a remark, but their circumstances had made him short-tempered, and he snapped back. "Well, I haven't heard you singing any happy songs, Dave."

Dave glared. "All you've done is gripe, and I'm telling you to shut up!"

Reb's face flushed. "I don't see anybody in here that can *make* me shut up!"

Dave had been keeping his temper under tight control, but now he threw himself onto Reb, driving him backward. The two fell and began hitting at each other, rolling on the floor.

Sarah jumped to her feet and grabbed Josh's arm. "Stop them, Josh!"

Josh shouted, "Cut that out!"

But the two combatants paid him no heed. They got to their feet, and Reb caught Dave over the eye with a blow that drove him into the wall. Dave struck out, catching Reb in the mouth.

Then Jake came up behind Reb and jumped on him. "Get hold of Dave, Josh!" he called out.

Josh thrust himself between the two. He started to say, "Now you two quit this." However, he had no chance, for in their anger both boys were unreasonable.

Dave's fist caught Josh on the chest and knocked the wind out of him.

Sarah and Abigail were both crying for them to stop.

Suddenly a voice said, "I bring you greetings of peace."

Startled, Reb and Dave dropped their arms, and everyone turned toward the dark end of the attic. A dim form could barely be discerned there.

Instantly Josh knew who it was. "Goel," he gasped.

The figure stepped forward, a tall man wearing a dark gray cloak that reached to the floor, with a cowl that covered his head. The lamplight illumined his stern features. "Why do I find you fighting among yourselves, my friends?" he asked, pushing the cowl back.

Reb ducked his head and muttered, "I'm sorry, Goel."

"Me too," Dave said, his face flushed with embarrassment. "I—I just lost my temper."

And then they all moved toward him, and he took each one firmly by the shoulders, greeting them all warmly —even Dave and Reb.

Finally Josh said, "I'm sorry you found us like this, Goel, but—"

"I know, my son." Goel nodded. "It has been hard." His gaze ran over the seven young people. Then a smile turned up the corners of his lips and gave him a kindly look. The sternness left him. "I have asked hard things of you—and now I have come to ask another hard thing."

Reb instantly said, "Just ask *anything!* I'd rather be doing something important than just sitting here."

Goel looked at him for a long moment. "My son, you must learn to wait. They also serve who only stand and wait. And the least of my servants, if they are faithful in what I command, are as great as the mightiest." He obviously saw that the boy did not understand. "One day you will learn this, Bob Lee—and it may be a hard lesson."

"What is it you want us to do?" Josh asked.

Goel looked long and hard at the Seven Sleepers. "You have a long journey to make—and a difficult task at the end of it. The Dark Power is sweeping over a small portion of Nuworld. Many years ago, after the old earth was destroyed, when all of you were placed in your sleep capsules, a man named Dion survived with some of his people. He led them far back into uninhabited places. There he founded a kingdom, and now that kingdom is in trouble. He is a good man, and his people are good people—but the Dark Lord and the servants of the Sanhedrin have already begun to destroy what he built up."

"What sort of a place is it?" Sarah asked timidly.

Goel asked, "You have heard of King Arthur and his knights of the round table?" When they all nodded, he

15

said, "Dion was a scholar studying medieval days. After the last great war, his mind was not steady. And when he built his kingdom, he built it after the ideas of King Arthur, even naming it Camelot." He paused. "When you get there you will see strange things. What you must remember is this—unless someone goes to help Dion, Camelot and all in it will fall under the sway of the Dark Lord!"

"We'll do it!" Reb exclaimed. "Just tell us how to get there."

Goel nodded. "I knew that you would, my son." His eyes swept over them. "I have great faith in you, and now you must have great faith in me, for your task will be difficult. Come now, let us talk, and I will tell you about Camelot . . ."

2

Journey to Camelot

Abbey shifted uncomfortably in the saddle and frowned. "I'm tired of riding all day every day—and I don't like this horse any more than she likes me!"

Reb was leading the procession. They were winding along a narrow trail enclosed on both sides by tall trees. For some time the path had been barely wide enough for one horse, but now it broadened.

Reining in his horse, Reb sidled up to the girl's and grinned. "Why, Abbey, this is nothing! You ought to have been with us back in Arkansas when we used to round up some of the wild pigs that roam the woods."

Abbey pouted, her full, lower lip protruding.

She was a beautiful girl, Reb thought, by far the prettiest girl he had ever seen. He admired her blue eyes, as angry as they now were.

"Why would I want to hunt stinky old pigs?" she snapped back. "Anyway, it seems to me we could have gotten to Camelot an easier way!" She shifted uncomfortably, which caused her gray mare to buck slightly. Grabbing at the saddle horn, she gasped and cried out, "Oh! I'm falling!"

Reb instantly spurred the bay he was riding so that he could grab the bridle of Abigail's mare. "You settle down there, girl!" he said sharply to the horse.

The mare gave him a cautious look and seemed to agree.

"See, all she needed was a good firm hand."

Abbey smiled at him with admiration, seeming to forget her irritation. "You're the best rider I ever saw, Reb! The rest of us can barely stay on, but you seem like you were just born in the saddle."

Reb flushed with pleasure. He, along with the rest of the boys, had been smitten with Abigail's good looks from the time she joined them.

Now he said, as modestly as he could, "Well, never was a horse couldn't be rode—never was a rider couldn't be throwed." He grinned broadly, his teeth very white in his tan face. "I guess I found a few of those that couldn't be rode, but I done pretty good at the rodeos."

"You were a rodeo star?"

"Well, I don't know about the 'star' part. I won the state championship in my age group two years running at bronco riding." As he thought back to those times, sadness crossed his face. "I did pretty good at steer wrestling too—but that's all gone."

He rode silently for a while, then glanced over his shoulder. The rest of the party was plodding along. The horses were weary with the day's long journey. Then he looked ahead and asked, "Do you ever wish we were back again where we used to be, Abbey?"

Giving him a startled look, she said, "Yes, I wish that almost all the time, Reb. But I didn't think you did."

"Why would you think that? I'm no different from anybody else."

Abbey could no more keep from flattering a member of the male species than she could keep from breathing. Besides, there was truth in what she said. "Oh, Reb, you are so self-sufficient! Of course, Josh is too, I suppose, and Dave and the others—but they're not like you. Why, look at how you've had to take over on this two-week trip! You had to teach us how to ride and how to take care of

18

the horses. And that map—why, you knew how to follow that even better than Josh and Dave did."

"Oh, I just been around horses more. Grew up with 'em, you might say. I had my own pony when I was only six and never got off a horse until . . ."

Abbey shot him a quick glance. "You mean until you went into the sleep capsule?" When he nodded, she sighed. "I know. I think of those days all the time. Oh, Reb, I had so much fun!"

"What kind of fun, Abbey?"

"Oh, parties—and I was a cheerleader and just getting real good at it. It was fun at school! I was elected class president—and I tried out for a part in a play. I would have gotten it too."

She thought about that time and shook her head sadly. "But that's all over now."

"I guess so. We can't go back."

The trees formed a living corridor of trunks that wound through the deep forest. The sun shone overhead and came down in filtered bars of yellow that made the riders blink. The deep silence of the woods was broken only by the occasional, far-off sound of birds. But more than once they surprised deer, which threw up their heads and bounded away.

Behind the two in the lead, the other five riders sat their horses in weary silence. They had risen at sunrise, cooked a quick breakfast, and traveled all morning. At midday they stopped to rest the horses and themselves, and they had eaten the cold sandwiches they had packed in their knapsacks. Now the sun was declining.

* * *

Josh kicked his horse into a trot until he was riding beside Sarah. "I hope we get to Camelot pretty soon. We're just about out of food."

19

"Well, according to the map we ought to be there tomorrow."

He gave her a strange look. "You know how maps are in Nuworld. Sometimes they work, and sometimes they don't." He looked back then. Jake seemed about ready to slip out of his saddle. He was exhausted. "Jake's not taking the trip well. Sometimes he's too tired to eat."

"I know. I feel the same way myself. We're just not used to riding this much." Sarah glanced ahead. "I wish we could all ride like Reb. He never gets tired."

"Well, he's kind of a cowboy," Josh said. "But anyway, let's just believe the map's right. Goel's never failed us yet."

At that moment a hawk flew overhead, crossing the sky almost like a bullet. Then it swooped suddenly to the earth, and there was the sound of thumping and a faint cry.

Sarah shuddered. "I know hawks have to kill to eat, but there's always something about it I don't like." Then she said, "No, Goel has never led us wrong." She looked at Josh carefully. "Are you afraid of what lies ahead of us in Camelot?"

Josh considered her words and shrugged. "Well, you might say I'm *apprehensive,* like when we went to Atlantis. None of us knew what to expect, and that's what we got—what we didn't expect. How do you suppose things are going back there?"

They talked about their adventure under the sea—about the king and queen and the other people they had met there and the exciting adventures.

Finally Josh said, "Well, I've had about all the adventure I need for a while."

"I guess all of us have—except maybe Reb—but we have to do what Goel says. Look, we've about reached the top of this mountain, haven't we?"

Josh noticed that the trail was widening even more. "Let's see if we've come to the peak." They spurred their horses to catch up with Reb and Abbey, and the beasts, as tired as they were, responded.

Soon all seven riders were racing toward the summit, which spread out into a much wider area. Minutes later they came to a sight that took their breath away.

A beautiful valley lay far below, like a green carpet. It was dotted with clumps of trees, and far away Josh could see dwelling places. His eyes were keener than the others', and he said, "See over there! That looks like a castle!"

As they all strained their eyes, Dave said, "I don't see anything, but I'm glad to be out of these woods." He looked down the forbidding slope. "The path down doesn't look like it's wide enough for a horse." He hated horses. "I think I'm going to walk down and let this beast get there the best way he can."

Reb laughed. "That hoss has surer feet than you, Dave. You better stay on board. Come on. I'm anxious to get down before dark."

As they descended, Jake moaned. "I'm gonna fall off this thing! Reminds me of a trip I took once. My folks took me to the Grand Canyon, and I had to get on a packhorse and ride down a trail like this. Only this one's steeper."

Josh, who was following closely behind Reb, did not like the steep incline to his right. The trail seemed to be carved out of rock and was solid enough, but it was very narrow.

For two hours the nerve-wracking descent continued until they finally reached the foot of the mountain.

Coming up beside Reb, Josh said wearily, "I'm glad that's over. Maybe we'd better camp—it's going to be dark in another hour."

Reb nodded. "I'll keep an eye out for a stream. Ya'll come on as you can."

Reb rode off. His big bay was seemingly as fresh as it had been that morning. Josh watched enviously as the boy guided the horse and sat on him as easily as if he were in a rocking chair.

They had plodded along for another fifteen minutes when suddenly Reb reappeared over to their right. He was riding at full speed.

Reb began waving. "Turn back! Get back into the woods!"

But it was too late. The horses began milling about, and Jake's horse suddenly hunched, throwing him to the ground. The boy grunted and then scrambled to his feet, trying to catch the animal.

By that time Reb had reached them. He wheeled his horse around to point in the direction of the woods. "Looky yonder—that must be some of the king's men. At least, I hope so!"

Josh followed the direction of the boy's gesture and received a shock. Half a dozen men were emerging from the woods. The sun glinted on their suits of bright armor, and the fading light caught the upright lances at rest in their hands.

"What'll we do, Josh?" Abbey cried out.

"Nothing. We couldn't outrun them on these horses even if they were fresh. Besides, why should we run? We were sent by Goel to the king."

Josh spoke with more assurance than he really felt. *Got to show some spunk here—even if I don't like the looks of those sharp lances.* He was thinking also that Goel had warned them about some knights in Camelot that were not to be trusted. "We've got no way of knowing who they are until we ask," he said. "Let's show them we're not afraid."

The armed men approached, widening their line and encircling the young people.

Dave whispered, "Wow, they look like they came right out of some movie! Look at them. All that armor!"

Josh was filled with apprehension, but he could not help but admire the beautifully wrought armor that gleamed like silver. All the men wore helmets with the visors down, and most of the helmets bore a streamer—red, yellow, blue—that caught the afternoon breeze. They carried swords at their sides, but at the moment each was pointing a steel-tipped wooden lance at the Sleepers.

One horseman nudged his charger forward a few feet, and his voice was muffled behind his visor. "Who are you, and what do you do in Camelot?"

Josh cried out loudly, "We are seven sent by Goel to King Dion!"

The leader swiftly raised his visor, and Josh took in the steady brown eyes that were examining him and the others.

After a long silence the knight said, "How can you prove this?"

Josh was somewhat taken aback. Goel had given them nothing to show that they were his servants, so Josh could only say, rather weakly, "When we talk to the king, we'll give the evidence. Take us there at once."

Another knight shook his lance in a threatening fashion. "They look to be spies to me. Let's hang 'em from the nearest tree."

A shiver ran over Josh, but he allowed nothing to show in his face. "If you hang the servants of Goel, woe be unto you."

The leader stopped the murmur that ran through the other knights surrounding them. He hesitated only for a moment more, then said, "I am Sir Gwin, one of the king's servants. We have had trouble with spies, and we must be

23

careful. Can you give no proof at all that you were sent by Goel?"

"We have no written message from him," Josh admitted. "If you'll let us talk to the king, I am sure he will be convinced."

Sir Gwin studied the boy, then nodded. "So be it. But you will have to give up your weapons, and you will be closely guarded."

The weapons, such as they were, were taken from them, and they were surrounded by a circle of knights, who eyed them warily.

As they made their way in the twilight, Sir Gwin said to Josh, "I hope you are telling the truth. If you are not, it will go ill for you."

"Why should we not be telling the truth?" Josh asked.

Sir Gwin turned to look at him. He had removed his helmet, revealing himself to be a handsome man with dark eyes and hair. "There are many who wish ill of the king. After all, he is the Sword of Camelot. We must be sure that you are not one of these ill-wishers. If you are from Goel, well enough, but if you are not . . ."

He shrugged, and his expression left no doubt in Josh's mind as to their fate.

Later Josh turned to Sarah. "I wish we had a letter or something from Goel. If we can't convince the king, they'll probably throw us in jail."

Sarah managed to smile, as tired as she was. "Well, we've been there before, and Goel never left us, did he?"

3

Another Dungeon

The journey to the castle they had seen in the far distance took several hours. Their horses were exhausted, and the Sleepers themselves were ready to drop. The sun quickly dipped behind the western mountains bringing darkness over the land. Only the pale, glowing moon that rose before them and the glittering stars enabled them to find their way.

Finally Josh asked wearily, "How much farther is it, Sir Gwin?"

"Not far. Less than a mile." The knight leaned closer to catch a glimpse of the boy's face. Surprisingly, he said, "I'm sorry to put you through this, my boy. I can see that you've all had a hard journey."

Sarah said, "You're just doing your job, Sir Gwin. We understand."

The knight's armor clattered as his horse jogged along. "We have to be careful. Better to be safe than to allow—" He broke off then and said no more until, some minutes later, he pointed ahead. "There, you can see the outlines of the castle. That's Camelot."

Josh looked up eagerly. Ahead the sky was broken by the outline of towering spires and the shape of what appeared to be castellated towers.

Then a challenge came out of the darkness. "Halt! Who goes there?"

"Sir Gwin on patrol with seven prisoners."

The knight led them past three armed men and over a drawbridge—it clattered loudly as it fell into place—and through the gates in a wall. When they were on firm ground inside, Sir Gwin held up his hand, and the group halted.

"Wait here, and I will see if the king will receive you." He dismounted and disappeared into the darkness.

Jake started to speak, but one of the knights said, "Keep your mouth shut! We won't have no spies' talk here!"

That cut back on conversation considerably, and they dismounted at the grumpy knight's command. He also commanded a man to take care of their horses.

Reb slapped his horse on the neck, saying, "Take good care of this one, will you, please?"

The groom shot him a suspicious look and led off the bay silently.

"Looks like everybody around here's suspicious!" Reb muttered to Wash. He looked up at the tower spires and shook his head. "I don't like the looks of this place."

"Me neither," said Wash. "Probably looks better in the daylight, though. I used to read stories about King Arthur. I always liked the pictures of the castles—but this one doesn't look so good tonight."

They waited a long time. When they attempted to sit down, Sir Elbert, the grumpy knight Sir Gwin had left in charge, snapped, "You can keep on your feet and don't have no talking among you." He walked carefully around them, carrying a naked sword that caught the gleam of the moonlight, and stopped in front of Josh. "One thing about it, if we find out you are spies, you won't have to worry about what to do with the rest of your life." He laughed heartily at his own words and nodded toward one of the other guards. "We know how to take care of spies and traitors around here, don't we, Sir Nolen?"

He started to say something else but was interrupted when Sir Gwin abruptly reappeared.

26

"Well, what did the king say?" Elbert demanded.

Sir Gwin gave the prisoners a look and shook his head regretfully. "The king isn't here. He and the royal family are on a visit to a neighboring castle. They won't be back for a while."

"But we have to see him!" Sarah said anxiously.

"Sorry about that, young woman," Sir Gwin said. "You'll have to wait until he comes back—and I'm afraid I'll have to keep you under guard." He turned and said, "Sir Elbert, see that they are placed in the dungeon."

"The *dungeon!*" several of the Sleepers cried.

Jake stepped forward and tilted his face upward to look into the face of the tall knight. "Why, you can't throw us into the dungeon—we're not criminals! I demand to see someone in authority!"

Sir Gwin looked down at the boy, and a smile touched the corners of his lips. "You've got spirit, young man. I like that. Nevertheless, until the king comes back we'll have to keep you in the dungeon. It's the law of the land. Take them away, Sir Elbert."

Elbert reached out and slapped Jake across the seat with the flat of his sword. "Get on with you now, and the rest of you too. Come on, Nolen, and watch 'em. If they try to run, use your sword and spit 'em like a roasted duck!"

* * *

"I suppose there are worse dungeons than this," Dave said, his voice tinged with disgust. "All the same, I'd like to get out of this place."

By standing on his bed he was able to see through the bars of the high window. The sun was now streaming through it. He had just reported what he saw—an open field where several men were engaged in martial exercise. Some were fencing with swords, while others on horseback aimed their lances at a small ring suspended from a post by a string.

Dave stepped down to the floor and put his hands on his hips, staring at Josh. "We've got to get out of this place, Josh," he urged. "Goel didn't send us here to rot in a dungeon!"

Josh was sitting on his own bunk looking at the floor gloomily. Lifting his head, he stared back at Dave. "Well, of course! Now why didn't I ever think of that? That's what we need—to get out of here. By george, Dave, you're a smart one."

Dave glared and plopped down on his cot. "You don't have to get funny about it. It's just that I'm sick of this place."

"Why, I reckon we all are." Reb was sitting at the cell's single table, across from Jake and Wash. The three of them were playing a game that Reb had made out of some paper left by a previous tenant.

Reb picked up the pitcher and poured himself a mug of tepid water. He took a long drink, stared at the mug distastefully, then set it down. "I thought I could bust out of just about any pokey in the world. But there's only that one door, barred and locked, and two guards there all the time." Then he stared over at Josh. "We just have to wait, I reckon, huh, Josh?"

They had been in the cell for two days now, and the time had worn on their nerves. The girls were being held in another cell whose location was unknown to them. Josh had demanded of Sir Gwin, who came to visit them every morning, that they be placed in better quarters. But this exceeded the knight's orders. Josh could tell that he was regretful, for he seemed a pleasant enough fellow. It was Sir Elbert who made life miserable for them.

"I'd like to hide that fellow Elbert under this jail so deep that they'd have to pipe sunlight to him!" Jake snorted. He was incensed at the treatment they had been receiving, and ten minutes later, when Sir Gwin stepped into the cell, he announced, "I have something to say." He stood up and placed himself pugnaciously in front of the tall knight, his hands on his hips and his dark eyes filled with determination.

"You usually do, Master Jake." Sir Gwin nodded. He seemed to have grown rather fond of the seven and had remarked that he would gladly have placed them in better quarters—except that he could not go against the king's law. "Say on, then."

Jake nodded and answered in a high, clear voice. "Sir Gwin, I'd planned to be a lawyer back in the old days. That's what my father was. He saw to it that people who were falsely accused got free from the law—and that's what I intend to do right now!"

"Very good." Sir Gwin nodded again. "Proceed."

Jake stared at him, taken a little aback. "I *am* proceeding," he said. "I'm telling you that we are not going to stay in this filthy cell any longer. I'm not going to put up with it!"

"It isn't exactly filthy," Gwin protested mildly. "We have it cleaned every morning, give you fresh water, food. As far as dungeons go, I could show you some that would make you cry to come back to this one."

"Be that as it may," Jake argued stubbornly, "I demand to see whoever is in charge of this whole castle."

Sir Gwin's wide mouth turned up in a grin. "His name is Melwitz, and you wouldn't like him at all. He's one of the senior counselors to King Dion, and I can guarantee that, if he knew you were here, he'd have you boiling over a slow fire."

Josh said hurriedly, "I don't think we want to go over your head, Sir Gwin. We'll just wait until the king returns." He whispered, "Now shut up, Jake, before you get us in *real* trouble!"

Sir Gwin shook his head regretfully. "I sent word to the king as soon as we brought you here, but he is sometimes difficult to find on these trips of his. He goes around from castle to castle, talking to different noblemen. Says he wants to keep his eye on the country and his finger on the pulse of what's going on, especially in these times."

"Can't you tell us a little about what *is* going on? Goel told us there was trouble," Josh said, "but he didn't say what."

Sir Gwin hesitated. "I'm not allowed to talk about such things—not until the king gives his permission. Nevertheless, I do have some good news for you. I'm arranging for you to have a little more outdoor exercise. I know these cells have gotten tiresome. Come along now."

The boys glanced at each other and scrambled to get through the door on the heels of Sir Gwin. He led them down a long passageway, then stepped outside, allowing them to follow. "There are your friends, the young ladies," he said. Even as he spoke, Josh looked across the yard and saw Abbey and Sarah standing beside three knights.

When they saw the boys, they came running.

Abbey's eyes were somewhat frightened, and she clung to Josh saying, "Oh, Josh, how much longer do we have to stay here?"

But Sarah said, "Don't be silly, Abbey! If it were up to Josh, we'd be out today." Then she smiled at him and asked, "Are you all right?"

Josh nodded. "Sure, it hasn't been bad. Just the idea of being in another dungeon doesn't appeal to me."

Sir Gwin was interested in Josh's choice of words. "*Another* dungeon?" he asked. "Do you young people make a habit of being thrown into dungeons?"

Josh shrugged. "When you serve Goel, it goes with the territory, I guess."

Sir Gwin bit his lip and stood looking at the group. "Well, for my own part I believe you—but it will be the king who will have to say. Come now—let me show you around part of Camelot at least."

"What are those fellows doing?" Reb asked when they had made their way to a large open area, somewhat like a football field.

He was looking toward several men on horseback who were in full armor and seemed to be practicing the same game that they had seen through the window of their cell.

"Why, they're practicing their tilting," Sir Gwin said. "Don't you know what that means?"

"Does it mean when they try to knock each other off their horses with them sticks?" Reb demanded.

"Well, that's not a very *graceful* way of putting it—but it's about what it amounts to. Don't they have such things where you come from?"

Josh said quickly, "I think we've all seen a little of it. But it's only on TV."

"TV?" Sir Gwin asked in a puzzled tone. "What is TV?"

Josh suddenly realized that in this culture they had no idea of television. "Just something we used to do. But tell us about the tiltings. We know the knights run at each other on horses and try to knock each other off. Do they get hurt?"

"Hurt! They get killed sometimes," Sir Gwin said in surprise. "Look. Sir Elbert and Sir Nolen—they are getting ready to have a try at it right now."

He motioned to where two men in armor were sitting on their horses facing each other and separated by a fence no more than three feet high.

"The fence is to keep the horses from running into each other," Sir Gwin explained. "See, they have to tilt their lances over the fence and try to knock their opponent off."

"Well, I hope whoever's fighting Sir Elbert knocks him all the way over the other side of the mountain!" Dave said bitterly.

"Sir Elbert is not pleasant." Sir Gwin shrugged. "But he's been unhappy in love. He was jilted by his sweetheart a couple of years ago, and he's still angry about it."

"He doesn't have to take it out on us!" Jake complained. "Look—they're starting!"

The Sleepers watched the scene with fascination. The two horses lunged forward, carrying the men toward each other. Each man held his lance pointed to his left, in front of a shield that he carried on his left arm to try to catch the opponent's lance. The knights came together with a clash, and Sir Elbert's opponent went sailing off the back of his horse. He fell to the ground with a clatter and rolled over several times.

"Is he dead?" Abbey gasped.

"Dead? Not a bit of it," Sir Gwin said cheerfully. "He just got knocked off his horse. See, he's getting up."

Reb had been watching the process with interest. "That's a mighty fine game," he said. "I wouldn't mind trying that myself someday."

Sir Gwin looked at him with approval. "If we don't cut your head off, I'll see to it that you get a chance to learn a little about the manly art of tilting. I think you might be good at it."

Then he took them through other parts of the castle, and they saw firsthand some further activities of the knights: practicing with the broadsword, fencing with lighter swords, and a great deal of horsemanship.

Finally, after an hour, Sir Gwin led them back to their cells. Abbey and Sarah were taken to their own room, and, as the five young men entered theirs, the door slammed behind them. For some time they said little, all of them deep in thought about what they had seen.

Supper came, which proved to be surprisingly good. Josh suspected that Sir Gwin had given orders to improve the menu. They sat around lingering over the meal, all of them looking depressed.

Finally Josh heard the sound of approaching footsteps. Then the bolt rattled in the heavy door, and it swung slowly open.

The man who entered looked like no one Josh had ever seen before. He was no more than medium height. He kept himself so straight, however, that he gave the impression of being taller. He was not young, nor even middle-aged, for his hair was silver-white, as was the short beard that covered the lower part of his face. He wore a simple garment, a gray outer cloak made of what appeared to be cotton or wool, and around his waist was a belt with a large buckle bearing a strange device. The cowl was thrown back from his head, exposing a pair of intense, pale blue eyes.

Josh looked into those eyes, and for one moment a thrill of fear shot through him. It was as though the old man had x-ray vision, for Josh could feel himself somehow being searched. It was as if someone were going through his pockets! The gaze of this strange man seemed to inspect his very soul. But then the fear passed, and Josh nodded. "How do you do? What are you being thrown into prison for?"

A smile touched the lips of the old man, barely visible beneath his mustache. "Oh, I'm not a prisoner. My name is Elendar."

Dave stared hard at the elderly man, who had strangely youthful features despite the silver hair and beard. "Are you come from the king?" he asked.

"Oh, indirectly, you might say that." The man who called himself Elendar stood examining each one of them. "May I know your names?" he asked politely.

He received them quietly, seeming to understand more than the bare syllables. Finally he said quietly, "If I may sit down, perhaps we could have a talk." He seemed not to be asking for permission, however, but seated himself at the table. "Now, I would like to hear a little more about you than just names."

Jake stood up pugnaciously, planted his feet, and stared defiantly at their visitor. "I'm not sure," he said loudly, "that we're ready to give our life history. We've been in this dungeon for three days begging for a chance to see the king or one of his representatives, and suddenly you appear. Are you a representative of the king of Camelot?"

Once again a glint of humor gleamed in the pale blue eyes, but he shook his head. "Not directly." He paused for one moment, then added, "I am the seer of King Dion's court."

"A seer?" Wash asked. "Does that mean that you do magic and stuff like that?"

"Oh, I am capable of a few things that you might call illusions," Elendar said, studying the small, young figure. "But I didn't come here to conjure up rabbits out of a hat. And you are right not to trust all strangers."

"Elendar, can you get us to the king?" Jake demanded.

"I think that might be arranged—but it might be better if you tell me your story first." He settled back in his chair and folded his hands quietly. "If you were brought directly before King Dion, you might find yourself in a great deal of difficulty. His Majesty is very suspicious of

34

strangers. If he were not satisfied that you were innocent, he might have you put to the rack in order to make you more talkative."

"Well, that won't be necessary," Josh said quickly. He had decided that this man was more than he seemed. "Let me explain . . ."

For fifteen minutes Josh sketched the history of the Seven Sleepers. He related also how they had encountered the Sanhedrin and Elmas, the Chief Interrogator, and had been used in the service of Goel since their arrival.

Elendar nodded. "Yes, Sir Gwin told me that you were the servants of Goel." He hesitated, then said, "I, too, am one of his servants in a small way."

"Then you do believe we are innocent of any wrong?" Dave asked quickly.

"Oh, yes, I knew that as soon as I looked into your faces." He laughed aloud, a surprisingly youthful laugh. "I may not do magic, but I have grown quite adept at reading the faces of men and women. I knew at once that you were really not of Nuworld. And now I am certain of it."

"When can we see the king?" Josh asked.

"In the morning. He will be here then." He saw the look on Wash's face and smiled. "Oh, that's not magic or foretelling. I have been gone on a long journey myself, and as soon as I returned I was told of your capture. Then a messenger arrived saying that King Dion and the royal family will be back tomorrow morning."

"What can you tell us about Camelot?" Dave asked. "We don't know anything except that there's some sort of trouble."

Elendar studied the five young men, and there was pain in his eyes. "This has been a very happy, peaceful place, this Camelot. King Dion's father had trouble with his mind, perhaps—but when he built the kingdom, at

35

least he copied a fairly good model. For if you know the story of King Arthur, you remember that he valued honesty, courage, and purity."

"We've read the stories," Josh said, "but the place still looks a little fantastic. Is this really like those days when King Arthur ruled a kingdom?"

"Pretty much. We have all the trappings of that society. We have knights and ladies and, believe it or not, even something very close to what were called 'dragons' in the old mythology—frightening beasts—some sort of mutant from the days after the Burning."

Suddenly Elendar arose, went to the door, and knocked. Turning, he said, "Tomorrow, then, you will meet the king. Afterward I am sure we will have more time."

The door opened, he left, it clanged shut.

Josh turned to the others and said with relief, "Well, I'm sure glad he's on our side!"

4

Trial by Combat

Elendar was prompt to keep his promise. At eleven o'clock the next day he appeared in their cell, announcing, "The royal family is waiting to receive you."

As Elendar led the boys out of their cell and turned right, Josh asked, "Have you talked to the king about us?"

"Yes. I have told him that you are to be trusted. However, the Sword of Camelot is a stubborn man and must make up his own mind."

He took them through a maze of corridors and up two flights of steps to a door that was guarded by two husky soldiers in armor. Without speaking to them, Elendar motioned, and they stepped aside. He entered, and the group followed him.

Josh looked around curiously, having time only to note that it was not an ornate room. There was a large table in the middle, where four people were seated. Against one wall stood a large cabinet, and the high windows were draped with crimson draperies having the name "Camelot" embroidered on them.

"Sire, these are the servants of Goel." Elendar called off their names.

And as he did, Josh studied the royal family.

The king was reaching old age. Like Elendar, he had silver hair, but his skin was wrinkled and his hands were not completely steady. He was tall and somewhat stooped, even at the table. However, he had a regal bearing that impressed Josh.

The queen—Queen Mauve—who sat beside him, was an attractive older woman with silver hair and brown eyes. She was younger than her husband apparently, and she watched them with interest.

Across from her sat two young people. The girl was introduced as Princess Elaine. She was, Josh thought, very beautiful, with blonde hair and blue eyes. Beside her, Prince Loren stared at them curiously. He had flaming red hair and dark blue eyes, and there was pride in his bearing.

"So, you claim to be the servants of Goel?" King Dion said in a strong voice. "But you have no evidence."

"N-no, Your Majesty," Josh stammered. "We had hoped to meet him here, and I'm sure he'll come eventually."

King Dion looked Josh over carefully. "In ordinary times this might be sufficient. However, these are not normal days."

Queen Mauve said, "I'm certain that they are who they say they are. They have honest faces."

But Prince Loren shook his head, and there was arrogance in his voice as he said, "How do we know *who* they are? They might have been sent straight by our enemies. I say let them prove themselves!"

Princess Elaine glanced at her brother and started to speak but then seemed to change her mind.

It was her father who answered. "Very apt, my son! We will try these young people. They look well enough, but appearances can be deceiving. Let there be a trial by combat."

Elendar protested, "But Your Majesty, these are not trained in our ways!"

"Then let them be so. The trial will take place in two days. You are free to leave. Stand not upon the order of your going."

Elendar bowed, and the Sleepers, noting this, did the same. There was some problem getting out without turning their backs upon the royal family, which would have been ill manners. However, Elendar led them outside and back down the corridors.

"I have found better accommodations for you." he said. "You don't have to go back to the dungeons."

"Well, that's a relief," Dave said. "I'm sick of that place."

"You'll still be under guard," Elendar warned. "Do not try to run away, for you would not get far." He took them to a hall broken by several doors. "Here. This will do for you young ladies," he said. "And this for you young men."

"What is this trial by combat?" Jake asked as they entered their quarters. "I know a little bit about trials, but the ones I'm familiar with usually have a jury."

Elendar shook his head. "I know not what is a jury. But in this country when there is a problem between two men, they fight. The winner is judged to be in the right."

"What about the loser?" Jake demanded.

Elendar smiled frostily. "Very often, Jake, he is dead, so he cares very little about the outcome. If he is merely wounded, his property is confiscated."

"But we don't know how to fight!" Wash piped up. "What chance would we have against armed knights?"

There was doubt in Elendar's eyes too. "That is the problem, Wash. But come inside, and we will talk. I am a very minor seer, but perhaps I can be of some help."

* * *

"It doesn't look like we have much hope, does it?" Sarah said. She was sitting with Dave beside a wall, watching as Sir Nolen engaged in swordplay with Reb.

The knight, who was rather small but very quick, fenced a blow that sent Reb's sword spinning. It caught the flashing light of the sun and fell to the ground, and Reb's face grew red with embarrassment.

"Well, what do they expect?" Dave complained. "These fellows have spent their whole lives practicing with swords and lances and such. Now, if they would just let us have long-range rifles or something like that . . ."

The two had been talking of what had occurred over the past forty-eight hours. Elendar had put them in the charge of Sir Nolen, telling him, "Find out which one would have the best chance, and with what weapon."

Easily said! But it had not worked out exactly that way. Even now they could hear Sir Elbert's high voice complaining, "Can't you even hold onto your sword? What do they *teach* you back where you come from?"

They had all tried their hands, except the girls, of course—even poor Wash, who was no match even for one of the other Sleepers. Obviously either Josh, Dave, or Reb would have to fight. Jake and Wash were both too small.

Sarah got to her feet, and Dave followed. They walked over to where Reb was standing, glaring at Sir Nolen.

"Don't feel bad, Reb," Dave said. "This just isn't your game."

Sir Nolen had discarded most of his armor. He was clad only in a gray overshirt, tight knit breeches, and short boots. "What *is* your game?" he demanded. He was almost in despair, for he was a friend of Elendar and had promised to come up with some answers.

The other Sleepers gathered around, and there was gloom in their faces.

Finally, Reb said, "It's pretty plain none of us are going to be able to match these fellows with a sword. It takes too long to learn. But I do have one idea."

40

"What is it?" Josh asked wearily. "Anything you can think of is better than what we've got!"

Reb bit his lip and glanced over toward where two knights were jousting. "I don't know about those lances," he said, "but I haven't seen anybody around here who can ride any better than I can."

"Is that right?" Sir Nolen demanded quickly. "I haven't even tried you on a joust. That's harder than swordplay."

"If its got something to do with a horse," Reb said stubbornly, "I'll take my chances."

Sir Nolen considered the tall young man and seemed to find something he liked in the light blue eyes. "All right, my boy. It looks like that's going to be our only hope. Come along, and we'll see how you do on a horse. You can use mine."

Reb and the others followed the small, cocky knight to the part of the court where the horses were stabled. "That's him—his name is Blaze," Nolen said proudly. "He's a bit of a handful."

Reb grinned at him. "'Never was a horse couldn't be rode,'" he quoted. "Just let me have a try."

Thirty minutes later Sir Nolen was whistling with amazement. "You are a fine rider, lad! I never saw better! Blaze doesn't take to everybody, but he likes you. I can see that. You've let him know who's the boss, and that's what counts with horses."

"I can ride him all right, but what about the rest of it?" Reb said.

"Well, that's the rub. You seem to be a pretty strong lad. Let's try you on the lance."

Soon Reb proved that he could put a lance tip through a six-inch ring, and again Sir Nolen was amazed. "Why, there's men that can't do that who've been jousting for years. Now, here's the important thing. You've got the lance in your right hand. What do you do with your left hand?"

"Why, guide the horse," Reb answered with surprise.

Sir Nolen laughed. "You hold a shield with it, boy! Otherwise, you'd get the other fellow's lance right through your gizzard. You steer the horse with your knees. Blaze is trained to do that. So now, let me give you this shield, and you try that."

Reb was a little disconcerted but soon found that the sturdy horse obeyed instantly any command he gave with his knees. One slight pressure, and the horse turned.

"Of course, there's no need to turn," Sir Nolen said. "You are headed straight along the fence. Your lance is pointed over it. You don't *want* your horse to turn."

"Well, I think I can handle this part of it," Reb said. But the thought of that lance coming straight at him troubled him. "How do I keep the other fellow from hitting me?"

"The helmet you will wear is made so that it will slip his lance if he goes for your head. There's nothing on it to catch. The trick is to shift your shield so that his lance goes off to the side. Then, with your own lance, go in over the top or side and catch him in the body. Come along. I'll mount up, and we'll run through it a few times."

That sounded simple enough, but Reb soon found that it was more difficult than it seemed. Sir Nolen upped the pace until finally they were galloping at each other at what seemed to be a furious rate.

Each time Reb learned something, and finally Sir Nolen said, "Well, boy, we can run at each other all week, but now we'd better try it for real."

He put on full armor and encased Reb in the same.

"Remember, catch the tip of my lance on your shield and try to catch me on the body."

"I feel clumsy as a possum in this tin suit!" Reb complained.

"Aye, we all feel the same. But we'd be dead without it. Come now, let's try it for real."

Reb guided his horse back to his end of the jousting field and turned him around.

Sir Nolen did the same.

Then Nolen shouted, "Go!"

Reb kicked Blaze into a gallop, and the two horses approached each other at breakneck speed.

Reb knew he could not out-joust a man such as Sir Nolen, who had made jousting his life, but he had an idea. As they drew close, he suddenly tilted his spear up toward Sir Nolen's head. Sir Nolen was not expecting that and flinched, which pulled his shield to one side. At the moment Sir Nolen's lance struck Reb's shield and slipped aside, Reb's own lance drove into the body of the knight, and he heard a crash as Sir Nolen fell to the ground.

He could not stop Blaze immediately, but he heard a cheer from the sidelines. Whirling his horse around, he looked back anxiously, and threw down his lance. He stepped off his horse and clanked back to Sir Nolen, afraid that he was hurt.

"Are you all right?" he asked.

Sir Nolen got to his feet awkwardly and shoved his visor back. Reb saw that he was grinning. "Yes, I'm all right. That was a neat trick, lad. That's exactly the one you'll use tomorrow against whatever champion the king appoints. Caught me off guard, it did, and it may work again."

* * *

When the trumpet sounded the next day, Elendar came to stand beside Reb, who was again mounted on

Blaze. At the far end of the jousting field, a very large knight in black armor was waiting.

"He looks as big as a house," Reb said. "I don't have much of a chance, do I, Elendar?"

Elendar's pale blue eyes seemed to glitter. "The battle is not always to the strong," he whispered. "Goel would not have sent you here and put you in this place if there were no chance. Now I'm no jouster, but I know that courage is the essential ingredient. Every knight will tell you—the man who flinches is the man who loses."

Reb looked over at the huge knight. The sun caught the tip of the man's lance as he held it high. He felt a moment of fear.

Elendar seemed to sense it. He slapped the boy's leg. "Never take counsel of your fears, my boy. Believe in Goel, and do not flinch. Will you do that?"

Reb swallowed hard and looked over to where his friends were gathered next to the royal family. A huge crowd had assembled, and now all the flags and pennants were flapping in the breeze.

He knew he had but a small chance of victory. The champion was a fierce warrior, Sir Hector, who had slain many men in battle and was the champion of the joust. The king had said, "If you can survive Sir Hector, I will believe that you are who you say."

Reb fought down the dark fear that rose in him, and suddenly a wave of hope came. He could not explain it. It did not have anything to do with the circumstances. He was almost certain to lose. Still, a strange sense of assurance welled up within. He looked down at Elendar. "You're right. I think I can do it, Elendar. He may spit me like a chicken for a barbecue, but he'll have to kill me to do it!"

"Good, lad! Now—" Elendar raised his hand and let it fall, and the herald by the king suddenly blew a blast on his trumpet.

Instantly Reb put his heels to Blaze and narrowed his attention to the black knight.

The rest of the world seemed blotted out for Reb. He ignored the bright colors—the reds, the blues, the greens of the ladies' dresses. He ignored the shouts that came from the onlookers. All he saw was a black shield and the visor of Sir Hector as the huge knight lowered his lance.

The two rushed toward each other, and all sounds too seemed to fade. Yet there was a clear voice that came not into his ear but into his heart. *Do not be afraid, Bob Lee, for you will not fail!*

Reb would never know whose that voice was, but it sounded much like the voice of Goel.

And then he was in front of the great knight. The gleaming lance tip came straight at him. He lifted his shield and at the same time pointed his own lance at the head of the black knight.

Sir Hector's reactions were fast, and he was not completely fooled. His lance struck Reb's shield and shook the boy to his backbone. Nevertheless, he lunged forward, and as Hector moved his shield three inches to the right, Reb lowered his point and caught the large man in the side.

He felt the shock as they met—and then the pressure was off, and he was past. Wheeling Blaze around, he saw Sir Hector lying flat on the ground and his horse galloping away. He became aware also of the silence of the crowd.

Pushing back his visor, Reb lifted his lance and shouted with all his might, "Goel forever!"

"Goel forever!" his friends cried. They came running out from the stands, and, as he fell from his horse, clanking mightily, he was surrounded.

"You did it, Reb! You did it!" Abigail cried. "There never was anything like it."

Josh said, "A real servant of Goel, Reb!"

Bob Lee Jackson knew that it had not been his doing. "Goel helped me," he said simply. "I guess if I ever doubted anything about him, I won't never do it again!"

5
Basic Training

I hardly know how to explain it," Elendar said.

He was sitting in the shade of a yew with Josh, Reb, and Sarah. The others had gone off to explore the castle again.

Elendar leaned back against the tree, his pale blue eyes half shut. He stroked his beard, while from the jousting field came the sound of crashing metal as a knight was knocked from his saddle.

Josh broke into Elendar's reverie. "Well, I don't understand why you don't just tell the king about Melchior."

Elendar had been telling how the forces of a knight named Melchior, who lived on the outer verge of the kingdom, had been swayed by the powers of the Sanhedrin. He also informed them that the king seemed unable to comprehend that Melchior was not to be trusted.

"I think sometimes," Elendar said quietly, "that Elmas has been able to cloud the mind of the king. I can no longer speak to him as freely as I once could."

"Why, that's just what happened in Atlantis!" Josh exclaimed. "It wasn't the king but one of his followers who got sort of hypnotized there." He went on to explain.

Elendar's eyes narrowed even more. "That's the work of the Dark Lord right enough. I've been on many long journeys, and everywhere I go the darkness seems to be creeping over the earth. Only Goel offers any hope."

"Does everyone here believe in Goel?" Sarah asked.

"Unfortunately not. The king does—and the queen—

but as I say, the king's judgment is clouded. Perhaps he's just getting old, as I am."

Reb considered Elendar, then shook his head. "I don't understand much about this. I'm just a good old country boy from Arkansas, but what is it Melchior does that is so bad?"

"It's not what he does so much as it is his influence," Elendar said grimly. "He's made himself very popular with many of the knights and the noblemen. They trust him—many of them—and he promises them great things." Angrily he shook his head, and a butterfly that had lighted on his white hair flew off. He watched it for a moment. "The time will come when the king will be sorry he's trusted Melchior—but I'm unable to get that across to him."

"Well—" Reb sighed "—I don't know anything about politics. My uncle was a county judge. He was a good man before he got that job, but it sure ruined him!"

Elendar smiled slightly, but there was a grimness in his face. "It was once said, 'Power corrupts and absolute power corrupts absolutely.'"

"But that isn't always true, is it?" Sarah asked. "I mean, Goel has power—and *he's* good. You have power, Elendar—and *you're* good."

"Some have not the ability to refuse what power brings with it. Melchior is one of those. He wants power for his own sake, whereas Goel uses his for the good of others—and I also, I trust." He shook himself and stood to his feet. "I'll leave you here now, but I hope you'll understand our ways a little better through these sessions we have." He turned quickly and left them.

Sarah said, "He's so wonderful! I never thought seers would be like that. I thought . . ."

Josh looked into the distance. "He's got power too, but I think he's afraid it's not enough."

* * *

"Boy, this is tough." Dave dropped with exhaustion to the ground. He had been fencing with Josh, and the two of them were puffing from the exercise.

Sir Nolen had stood near them, giving either who lagged the flat of his sword on the bottom.

Josh felt that his arms were going to fall off and was relieved when the knight said, "That'll do for now, but I'll be back in twenty minutes for more practice."

The young men had been practicing for days now. They had struggled with every kind of hand-held medieval weapon imaginable—knife, broadsword, foil, rapier, pike, halberd, and always, of course, the lance on horseback.

Dave and Josh were able to sit on a horse after a fashion but never had shown any talent for jousting. It was Reb who still excelled at this, growing more skilled each day. Wash and Jake floundered around with smaller weapons, never doing any damage to anyone—except that Jake once put a dagger through his own leg.

As the two boys rested, Dave said, "This looks kind of silly, doesn't it, Josh? I mean, how are we kids going to become warriors who can match the skill of grown men? We can't hope to beat experienced adult enemies."

Josh wiped the sweat from his forehead and lay back, shading his eyes with his hand. "I don't know, Dave, but you remember the high place where the Sanhedrin had us trapped? We did pretty well then."

"Yes, I remember that," Dave nodded, "but I just don't know what to expect this time."

"None of us do," Josh said. He looked up to see Sir Gwin coming and got to his feet.

Dave got up also. "I hope you've come to give us some book lessons. My arm's about to fall out of its socket."

Sir Gwin was wearing hose and a green doublet with slashes and a small black cap. "As you see," he said, grinning, "I'm not wearing armor. It's time for another kind of lesson. Come along. I've told Sir Nolen."

He took them first to their own quarters where they washed as well as they could. Then they were furnished some clothes of the same type that Sir Gwin wore.

When they were dressed, Gwin said, "The others are already waiting for us. We'll go now."

As he led them down the hall and up a flight of stairs, Josh asked, "What sort of thing will we be learning now? Which fork to use?"

Sir Gwin stared at him. "What's a fork?"

Josh blinked. "Why . . . uh . . . it's what you use to eat your food with!"

"Oh, we call that a knife here."

Dave laughed aloud and winked at Josh. "That's what we call it too, and we've been making out fine without forks since we got here." As they walked, he explained the nature of a fork, but when they got to the door of a large hall, Sir Gwin said, "Sounds like foolishness to me. If you've got a knife, you cut off the meat, stab it with the end, stick it in your mouth. That's all there is to it."

Josh winked at Dave. "You may be right."

They entered and found their friends waiting for them.

Abigail leaped up at once. "Oh, you finally got here. Now we can begin."

"Begin what?" Josh asked.

"Why, to learn to dance," Abigail said in surprise. "Didn't Sir Gwin tell you?"

"No, I was explaining to them that a knife is all one needs to eat with," Sir Gwin said. Then turning to Dave and Josh, he said, "This lesson will be in the more civilized things. For example, every nobleman of breeding must know how to dance."

Josh had sudden memories of falling over his feet back in Oldworld, and his heart sank. "Can't I skip that one, Sir Gwin? I'm not very good at it."

"No, you cannot," Gwin insisted. "You will learn to dance just as you have learned to fence. Musicians—"

Soft music filled the room as the three musicians at one end of the hall began to pluck harps and a lyre.

Sarah came up to Josh. "I'll show you how, Josh. It's easy. I've already been practicing."

Josh groaned. Ten minutes later, after stepping all over Sarah's feet, he said, "I'd rather be bashing somebody with a sword."

"You're doing fine," Sarah said firmly. "Now, put your right foot here . . ."

The dancing lesson seemed to go on forever, and after it was over, Sir Gwin sat them down and began to explain the other niceties of knighthood.

They all listened carefully, but Jake interrupted several times to protest that it sounded like foolishness to him. His small, round face looked disgusted. "I don't see how this is going to save Camelot, dancing around. Why don't we get on with the real thing?"

Sir Gwin smiled and answered, "This is the real thing, Jake. Being a knight involves many things. It's more than a matter of physical strength and skill with the lance, although that's part of it. For example, it is a knight's bounden duty to help those who are weaker."

"I like that," Sarah said. "That's a noble thing."

"It is also required of all knights that they treat women with gentleness and courtesy."

"I like *that*," Abigail said. She put an elbow into Dave's side, making him grunt. "You listen to this carefully—it's important."

He glared at her, but she smiled sweetly.

51

They listened as Sir Gwin explained the code of chivalry, which involved a complicated ritual.

At one point Reb broke out in astonishment. "What's that you say? It's all right for a knight to fall in love with a woman even if she's married?"

"Oh, yes." Sir Gwin shrugged. "According to our knightly code, a man may carry a woman's favor—that is, a silk scarf—on his lance in battle, even if she's married. All it's saying is that he admires her grace and beauty."

"Does it ever go—well—*farther* than that?" Sarah demanded.

Sir Gwin stared at her sternly. "I can't say that it *never* does. But true knights would never take advantage of a woman in any way."

The lesson went on for a considerable time, and when it was over Josh was ready to quit. He threw up his hands and cried out, "Stop! I'm going to have to learn how to behave all over again!"

"Well, it wouldn't hurt you," Abigail snapped. "You could stand a little more politeness."

Jake laughed aloud. "That's right, you pay attention to Sir Gwin. I'm expecting great things from you."

When they went back to their room, Josh slumped down in a chair and stared glumly at the other three boys. "I never heard of such! Goel sends us here to do a dangerous job, and we learn to go around kissing a girl's hand. Disgusting!"

"Oh, I don't know," Dave said with a smirk. "I didn't think it was so bad."

Jake picked up a pillow and threw it at him. It struck Dave in the face, and he yelped. "You wouldn't," Jake said. "You always were a ladies' man, Dave."

Dave threw the pillow back. "Looks like that's the thing to be around here." He looked over at Reb and asked, "Are you getting tired of all this business, Reb?"

Reb had a rather serious look on his face. "You know," he said, "I'm not. I guess I didn't know how much I'd missed a good horse. Of course, it goes with the territory, trying to knock somebody off with a stick, but I love that horse!"

He'd been given his own horse now and spent hours grooming him.

"You're our hope, Reb," Josh said. "All the rest of us can barely stay on one of those things."

Reb leaned back in his chair, laced his fingers behind his head, and said quietly, "I'll—I'll do the best I can—and that's all a bluenosed mule can do!"

6

A Home in the Forest

Life at Camelot went on pleasantly for the young visitors. The lessons in chivalry continued, though, much to the disgust of Josh—and to the delight of the two girls.

There was, they soon discovered, an entire code of chivalry. If a woman liked a knight, she would wear a certain flower in a certain position in her hair. The knight recognized this at once as a message that he was to continue his pursuit.

"Oh, I think it is so exciting," Abigail said. "Don't you, Reb?"

The tall blond boy glanced at her and grinned slightly. "Well," he drawled, "I suppose for girls it's all right."

The Sleepers were riding along a forest path. Elendar had encouraged them to travel as much as possible to learn the lay of the land. "You never know," he said, "when you'll need to find your way quickly. When trouble comes, it will come like lightning."

They had left the castle early that morning, had ridden long, and now, as the sun was high in the sky, had grown hungry.

Jake said, "Look, there's a little house over there. Maybe we can buy something to eat."

Josh shook his head. "They don't use money here, Jake—not very much. At least the poor people don't. Though we could trade them something. I'm hungry myself. Let's go have a look."

The shack they approached, Josh saw, was not impressive. Like the houses of most of the poor people, it was small, made out of several kinds of material such as clay and wattle, and crowned with the inevitable thatched roof.

As they entered the cleared area that lay behind the house, a group of children scattered. Two of them hid behind their mother, who had come out to stare at the visitors.

The man who was plowing in the field stopped the oxen and came running to them. He was a little man with a thatch of coal-colored hair. He was undersized, as were all the people in this world, and he yanked off his cap and tugged at his forelock in a gesture of submission. "Good day, kind sirs. Be ye lost in the forest?"

"Oh, no," Josh said, "we're just out for a ride." He looked doubtfully at the man and then glanced over at the woman. Fear was in her eyes. *I wonder what she's afraid of?* he asked himself. Aloud he said, "I wonder if we might rest awhile here? We are thirsty, and perhaps you might sell us some food."

The man cast a curious glance at the seven, then said, "Certain, sir. If you'll get off, I'll feed and water your horses."

Slipping to the ground, Sarah said, "Oh, this feels good!" She stamped her feet and arched her back and groaned. "I don't see how you ride all day, Reb, without getting stiff and sore."

Wash whispered to Jake, "This sure is a poor-looking farm! Back home even the poorest farmer in the county would have a better place than this!"

"It's pretty bad all right," Jake agreed. He looked about at the primitive house and at the few tools by the shed that seemed to serve as a barn. "We have to be careful not to hurt their feelings."

The woman came forward timidly. "We don't have much, but I'll fix what we have."

"Oh, anything will be fine, ma'am," Dave said quickly. "We're not fussy about what we eat."

The man had been watching. He introduced himself, saying, "My name is Will, and this is my wife, Donna."

The Sleepers smiled, and Sarah asked, "And what are the names of your children?" She listened carefully as the woman named them off. Then she repeated their names, saying, "I bet I have a game you four would like to play."

"A game?" the oldest said, a boy about eight. He was dirty, as were the others, but bright-eyed, and he asked eagerly, "What kind of a game?"

"It's called hide-and-seek. Do you know that game?"

"No." The boy shook his head. "I never heard of it."

"Come along. I'll teach you how to play."

As they moved away, the man Will said, "Make yourself to home. I'll be back soon."

His wife stared at him as he walked over to the shed and picked up a bow and a quiver of arrows. "Will, you can't—"

"Quiet ,woman!" Will said sternly. "We have guests. I'll see that they have something to eat, or my name ain't Will Temple." He nodded at his guests. "It'll take a while —but if you'll wait, I'll give you a supper fit for a king."

"Why, don't go to any trouble for us," Josh protested.

"No trouble, masters. The woods hereabout is thick with game. I'll be back in thirty minutes or an hour. My wife here will cook you a fine meal." He turned and disappeared almost at once into the depths of the forest that surrounded the small farm.

"That's almost like going to the grocery store," Jake grinned. "Just step out in the woods, kill a squirrel or rabbit or something, and come home."

"Not quite that easy," Josh said. "You've got to be able to hit something with that bow and arrow." He looked at the woman curiously—she seemed extremely nervous. Josh decided that she was overwhelmed with so much company and said, "Don't worry about us, ma'am, we'll just wander around and look things over until your husband gets back."

She bit her lip, then turned back to the house.

"I wonder what's wrong with her?" Abigail said. "She looks really frightened."

"Just not used to company," Dave guessed. "These people are very backward here. I guess we are nobility to them." He looked about him. "Look, let's stretch our legs. I'm tired of these horses."

He led the boys into the woods. As Will had told them, the forest was full of game, and Dave said, "If I'd brought my bow, I might even hit one of those rabbits."

They had a fine time that afternoon, although they were hungry. Finally, Josh said, "Let's go back. I think Will might have found our lunch by now." He led the way back and, sure enough, saw smoke rising from the chimney. "Soup's on," he said. "Let's go see what's for dinner."

When they reached the house, Will was working on the carcass of a deer, strung up by its heels, cutting it into pieces.

Will grinned, exposing rather bad teeth. "Ah, masters, you're back." He motioned to the deer carcass. "A fine fat buck! Donna's cooking up a haunch of it. Should be ready any time."

Thirty minutes later, the seven were all seated outside, eating off whatever was handy. There were only four wooden plates. The rest used pieces of board. The meat itself was delicious.

"My, this is so *good!*" Sarah said. She bit off a huge chunk and chewed it thoroughly. Then she drank a mug full of water, fresh from the spring. "I never had a better meal at McDonald's—not even a 'Happy Meal'—did you, Abigail?"

Abigail's face was usually immaculate, but now it was smeared with grease, and her bright hair was somewhat clouded by the smoke from the fireplace. The two girls had watched the meal being prepared, which consisted of shoving the meat on spits over the open fire until it was practically burned on the outside and still raw on the inside. But she smiled and said, "No, never. This is fine!"

The meat was supplemented with baked potatoes they had to pick at carefully to keep from burning fingers or lips. The Sleepers enjoyed their meal.

By now, the children had lost their fear of the young people and came close to ask many questions, mostly about Camelot.

"I'm going to be a knight when I grow up," the oldest boy, a lad named Robin, said confidently.

"No, you won't be no knight, lad," Will Temple said. "You have to be born to be that. You'll be a serf, just like me."

Josh looked up suddenly and said, "There comes Elendar! I wonder if he's got news from Camelot."

The silver-haired man rode up on a beautiful white mare, pulled her down, then got off. He beamed. "I see you're out getting to know the people of our country. Do you suppose I could have a bite of that meat?"

At once Donna scurried around. "Yes, sir, surely. There's plenty." She fetched him a portion, and Elendar sat down on a three-legged stool and listened as the young people gave him a report of their activities.

John noticed that Elendar's eyes went from one of the seven to another, and that he seemed to be evaluating them as if testing them in his mind. His sharp eyes never stopped. Then he looked up and said, "I hear horses coming."

Reb said in astonishment, "You sure do have good ears!" He listened hard and nodded. "But you're right—sounds like a whole army!"

His words were not far from wrong. A group of horsemen appeared, approaching from the direction opposite the way the Sleepers had come.

"It's the king," Elendar said. "He left early this morning to go out hunting." He got to his feet quickly, as did the others, and when the party halted he said, "Good day, Sire. Did you have a good hunt?"

King Dion's face was stern. He cast his eyes around the homestead, and they came to rest on the partly dressed-out carcass of the deer. He said, "Who has killed the king's deer?"

A silence fell over the group. Nothing was heard for a moment. Then Will's wife began to sob.

"Hush your crying, woman," King Dion commanded. He turned to Will Temple, who was standing still, looking at the king, and demanded, "Did you kill that deer?"

Will bowed in submission and said, "Yes, Your Majesty. I must confess. It was my arrow that brought him down."

"You know the penalty for killing the king's deer?"

Will hesitated, and there was a catch in his voice as he answered, "Yes, Sire."

"Take him," the king said, and at once two armed knights dismounted and advanced toward the small farmer.

Josh was alarmed and stepped forward. "Your Majesty, please—let me explain."

"*Explain?*" King Dion snapped. "There's no explanation, young man. The law has been broken, and the penalty must be paid."

"Penalty? Is there a fine?" Jake asked.

"A fine? I know not what is a fine." King Dion's eyes went back to Will, and they were filled with anger. "All well know what the penalty is for killing the king's deer. Any man who commits such a crime will have his right hand cut off."

"Oh, no!" Sarah gasped and stared in horror at the king. "You can't mean that, Your Majesty!"

The king had grown fond of the young people. But there was wrath in his face now, for he was jealous of his royal authority. He was also accustomed to violence and harsh penalties.

"You do not understand, young woman. There must be law in my kingdom. If there were not, what would we have? Every man would be an outlaw, taking what he pleased. The deer belong to the king. That is the law of the country. Only with the king's permission can anyone kill one."

Josh was dumbfounded. He had heard that the laws of the medieval world were strict and harsh—but he had never encountered anything like this. "Sire," he said, "the man did but try to be hospitable to us. It is our fault. He killed the deer to feed us."

King Dion shook his head. "He should have gotten permission. I would have granted it—but now it is too late." He nodded at the knights and said, "Proceed."

One knight pulled the trembling farmer over to a small table outside the storage shed and held his arm down. The other drew a gleaming sword. He tested its edge, then said, "I am ready, Sire."

Josh felt terrible. He whispered to Elendar, "We can't let this happen. It is all our fault."

Elendar stared at him curiously. "The laws are different here, my boy. I can do nothing."

Josh saw that Sarah was looking at him, a pleading look in her eye. He at once advanced to stand before the king and looked up into his face, "Sire, this cannot be."

"*Cannot* be? You dare to say 'cannot' to the Sword of Camelot?"

Josh said, "I would not offend Your Majesty. I am but a stranger here, but surely Your Majesty understands that no true man would want another to suffer for *his* wrongdoing. I beg you, sir, if someone must suffer for the offense—" Josh's eyes met the king's steadily "—let it be me. The fault was mine. The penalty should be mine."

A murmur ran around the knights who were watching, and Sarah said, "Oh, no, Josh!"

But he stood fast, held up his hand, and said, "If the fault was mine, the penalty must be mine, Your Majesty."

Nothing like this had ever come into King Dion's experience. His silver hair gleamed in the afternoon sun, and his dark blue eyes searched the young man. He was still a tall man and strong, though not what he had been in his youth. For a long moment he let the silence run on, and then he suddenly smiled. "You have courage, Joshua. I like that. A bit rash, perhaps," he added wryly, "but it is a good thing for a young man to be impetuous. I was the same myself when I was your age." He glanced at the two knights and said, "Release the man."

When the knights released Will, he straightened up, and his eyes went to Joshua. He whispered, "Thank you, sir. Thank you!"

His wife threw her arms around him.

Josh felt rewarded for the sacrifice he had offered to make.

"Well, you've had enough adventure for one day. Come along with me," the king commanded. "We have things to talk about." He waited until the seven were back on their horses and then rode out with his retinue of knights behind him.

Will came forward as Josh mounted, and he raised his hand. When Josh took it, there were tears in Will's eyes.

"Thankee, young master. Ye saved my hand for me. Maybe I can do something for you someday."

Josh smiled down at him, leaned over, and squeezed his hand. "It really *was* my fault, but I'm glad nothing came of it." He nodded and spurred his horse.

Sarah was waiting for him. As they rode on, she suddenly leaned over and grabbed him. Josh swayed in the saddle toward her, and before he knew what she was up to, she had planted a kiss right on his cheek with a loud smack.

"There, Josh! *That's* what a lady of Camelot does when her knight has done a noble deed!" She laughed at the flush in his cheeks. "Be careful that you're not so noble next time, or you may get more of the same!"

7

A Dangerous Hunt

I don't know if you've ever hunted anything quite so dangerous," Loren said.

The Sleepers were standing with the prince in front of the castle. The day was sunny and beautiful, and yet there was a worried look in the eyes of some of them. They listened apprehensively as Loren went on.

"You see, we hunt the wild pigs on foot." His eyes gleamed as he took in the faces of the boys. "And it takes a pretty good man to stand up to one of those beasts, I can tell you for sure!"

Reb looked at him curiously, then shrugged. "Well, I spent a lot of my time feeding pigs back in Arkansas. They didn't seem too dangerous to me."

The prince was wearing a buckram outfit and stood tall and strong in the sunlight. "I never heard of Arkansas," he said, "but the pigs around Camelot are about as dangerous a beast as you'll be likely to find." He held up his forefinger. "They've got razor-sharp yellow tusks this long. Let one of them get you down, and he'll unseam you from belly to throat."

Jake said nervously, "I think I'll just watch this time. No sense rushing into anything."

Wash grinned, his teeth very white against his black face. "Let's both of us watch. Reb, you know so much about pigs, we'll let you do the hunting."

Reb gave him a disgusted look. "The day I run away from a little old pig, that's the day you can put me on the floor!" he said defiantly. He was wearing a green doublet today, green breeches, and a pair of soft leather boots—the sort of outfit the boys were all wearing—and he gave Abigail a slight smile. "Hey, Abbey, I'm gonna show you how to get pork chops for supper!"

Loren looked at him with a superior expression. "Well, we'll just let you go on in the front of the hunters, then, Reb. You can show the rest of us how to do it."

Soon the hunters were in the midst of the forest. The king had come along too. He himself did not hunt, but he liked to watch his son and the other knights in action.

As they moved deeper into the woods, Josh looked around nervously. "This is one time I wouldn't mind wearing one of those tin suits," he said.

The king smiled at him. He had obviously grown to like the boy, mostly because of his offer to take Will's penalty a few days earlier. "You wouldn't be able to do much with a suit of armor on," he said jovially. "Those beasts are fast as lightning, so I want you young men to be very careful."

"Reb here has offered to lead the hunt." Loren grinned at his father. "I think that's fine of him, don't you?"

The king gave him a sharp look and shook his head. "It's not wise to let an untried hunter go up against one of those tuskers. You know how vicious they are, my boy."

Reb's pride was touched. "Don't worry, Your Majesty. I know how to handle pigs."

As they moved on, the ladies of the court joined them. The queen had been brought in a sort of covered cot, carried by two stout men. The young ladies walked along beside the canopy and listened as she told them of hunts in days gone by.

Reb dropped back and found himself walking beside the Princess Elaine. She was only one year older than he and seemed to be a merry young lady.

"Tell me about Atlantis," Elaine said. "It must have been frightening to go under the sea. I don't see how you could do it."

Reb shoved his soft cap back on his head. It had a pointed eagle's feather in it, and he took it off to admire it. "Aw, shucks," he said, "it wasn't so much, except when the big octopus pinned us down."

Elaine's eyes grew large. "An octopus! What's an octopus?"

"Big critter, with eight arms. This one had a beak big enough to snap your leg off." He launched into the tale of how the seven of them had been trapped in an underwater cavern by a huge squid. When Elaine looked at him with admiring eyes, he was forced to say, "Of course, it was Wash there that got us out."

"The little fellow?" Elaine said in surprise. "He doesn't look as though he could do a thing like that."

"Well, he says Goel was with him, and I guess that's what saved our bacon."

"Saved your bacon?" Elaine asked in confusion. "What does bacon have to do with Atlantis?"

Elaine listened as Reb explained the figure of speech, then walked along without speaking for a time. She clearly admired the tall young man, and her eyes went back to him as she said, "Tell me about Goel. Have you ever met him?"

"Met him!" Reb looked at her in amazement. "Why, of course I've met him." He told her how they had come out of the sleep capsules and been directed by Goel ever since. "I guess we're kind of his helpers, you might say. This Sanhedrin's a bad bunch." He wagged his head dolefully. "I understand they're trying to take over Camelot too."

Elaine's lovely eyes clouded, and she smoothed her hair back. "Yes, things have been difficult lately. More and more of our people are being drawn, I think, into the power of the Dark Lord."

She stepped even closer and put a hand lightly on his arm. When she looked up at him, her face was filled with apprehension, and she bit her full lower lip. "Do you think you and the others will be able to do something?"

Reb had always been a modest young man, but his experience at Camelot had not fostered this. Ever since they had left Atlantis, because he was an expert horseman and the travel had been on horseback, he had been more or less in a leadership position. And because he had become an expert jouster, tossing from their saddles some of the best knights, men who were far more experienced, this had given him a rather cocky air.

Now he did what he would never have done earlier. He waved his hand in the air and said, "Why, don't you fret none about it, Miss Elaine! I'll see to it that nothing happens to you or your family!"

Elaine blinked—and he noticed how long and thick her lashes were and how smooth her skin.

"Oh, that's so good to hear," she said as she squeezed his arm. "I'm so glad you came."

* * *

Reb enjoyed his talk with the princess, totally unaware of how boastful he had become.

Josh noticed, however, and whispered to Dave, "I think Reb's getting sort of a big head. I'm a little bit worried about him. One thing we don't need on this trip is a big fat ego to keep up with."

Dave agreed. "You're right, Josh. And I don't like this wild tusker business either. These wild pigs aren't anything to fool with."

Abigail had been listening in, and she sniffed. "You two are just jealous because Reb isn't afraid of anything."

Josh gave her a disgusted look. "It's good sense to be afraid of *some* things."

They moved on without saying more about Reb's problem.

Soon one of the scouts came running back, his face red with excitement. "Your Majesty," he said, "there's a huge tusker over there in that clump of trees!"

The king looked at Prince Loren. "All right, my boy, suppose you show your father what a fine hunter you are."

"I'll do my best, Sire." He gestured to several of the servants, who came forward bearing a sheaf of spears. Plucking one out, he motioned the guests forward. "This is what we use to hunt the wild boar. You four each take one, and you ladies can watch the fight."

Reb took a smooth, wooden-shafted spear. He touched the pointed blade on the end. "This thing is sharp as a razor. My Uncle Seedy, the barber, could shave with one of these things!" Then he looked at the extended blades on the side. These stuck out at right angles and were rather dull. "What are these things for?"

Loren held up his spear. "What you have to do is get this point into the boar." His eyes shone, and his lips turned up in a grin. "But I'm telling you, these boars are tough. They'll run right up the spear and gore you to death before you can blink."

"That doesn't sound like too much fun," Dave muttered. "But what are these side pieces for?"

"Here's what you must do," Loren said, demonstrating. "Shove the butt end of it into the earth. Nobody's strong enough to keep a three-hundred-pound boar at bay, so when he comes at you, let him run himself right onto this pointed blade. It'll go in up to the hilt, all the way up to these side blades, and that's what will hold him there."

Reb examined the spear and swallowed hard. Boar hunting began to seem more difficult to him. "Well," he said, "what happens then?"

Loren patted his spear, "You either stop him, or he pushes you back and gets you. Usually there's no third alternative."

Reb felt the eyes of the others on him and wished he had not been quite so bold, but it was too late now. "All right," he said, "I think I'm ready."

Loren began to deploy them. "Fan out," he said. "We don't know exactly where he'll charge from. You ladies stay back with the king and queen."

The hunters spread out in a long line and began to watch the forest nervously.

As Reb looked over his shoulder he saw that the king and queen, as well as the young ladies, were following rather closely. "Don't they need to stay back?" he asked Loren.

The prince grinned broadly. "Not as long as a stout fellow like you is in front to keep the boar off them," he jibed. Then he suddenly shouted, "Look! There he comes!"

Reb turned toward the most enormous pig he had ever seen. It came tearing out of the woods, running at full speed, and its eyes were red with fury. It was only a few feet to Reb's left, so he began to move in that direction. "I've got him," he yelled.

"Be careful!" Loren shouted. "Don't let him get through!" But he had no sooner yelled than the pig shifted direction and charged straight at one of the knights.

The knight was slow, and, even as the group watched in horror, the pig struck him. The boar's head flew up, and he ripped the man's leg from ankle to thigh. The man screamed. The pig next caught the man in the side. Then, apparently, he noticed the movement of the king and queen as they tried to retreat.

"Watch out! He's going for the king!" Sir Gwin shouted. "Watch him! Get him!"

Reb saw that Loren, who was on his right, and Dave,

who was on his left, were too far away. The pig was going to pass very close to Reb himself.

"Got to stop that sucker!" he mumbled. He stepped quickly into the pig's path. He could see the white froth on the boar's lips, and the yellowed tusks looked ten inches long. He vaguely heard people screaming, and someone cried, "Look, the king has fallen!"

Whipping a glance behind him, Reb saw the king sprawled on the ground and the queen trying to help him to his feet. *They'll never make it,* Reb thought. *It's up to me!*

It seemed as though time stopped, but he remembered one thing Loren had said. *Put the butt of the spear in the dirt—let the boar run onto it.*

He dug the hilt into the hard ground with both hands held firmly, and then the mighty boar was upon him! Its red eyes flashed with rage. Its mouth was open so wide he could count the teeth. Its bristles stood out as though electrified. And then the boar struck the end of his spear.

Though it took all his might, Reb held on. But the shock drove him backward, and the spear came loose from the earth. Now he had only his strength to hold off the pig. He felt like a pygmy as the boar roared toward him, snorting angrily.

"Got to hold him," Reb panted.

Then the boar threw itself to one side, and the spear in Reb's hands twisted mightily, sprawling him in the dust. He held on, breathing a quick cry for help. *O Goel, don't let that pig get at the king!*

It was a close thing. The spear had penetrated the boar's chest. He was wounded. But he still had plenty of fight left in him.

Then, with a surge of strength Reb had not known he had, he got to his feet and wrenched the spear loose.

He heard a cry of fear from the women and a shout of

warning from Loren. *"Don't let him off!"* The prince's voice seemed far away, but Reb knew what he had to do.

"Got to get him right in the throat." He drew the spear back and, as the boar launched himself again, took aim. And the razor-sharp blade found its target. Reb was thrown to one side, and he felt the rip of a mighty tusk along one forearm as the spear fell from his hands.

He's got me—I'm a goner! he thought wildly. The boar's heavy weight fell on him, and he gave up all hope.

Then the weight was being lifted, and through the mist he heard Josh saying, "You all right, Reb?"

Reb sat up and wiped the blood from his face. "He must have torn my head off," he said dazedly.

"That's not your blood," Loren said, awe on his face. "That's the boar's blood."

By this time, King Dion was there with the queen. "How is he?" the king asked anxiously.

"I'm all right, I reckon," Reb said thickly. But then pain stabbed his arm, and he held it up. "I did get nicked a little here."

Princess Elaine knelt beside him. "We've got to tie that up. He's bleeding badly."

Reb sat looking at the huge pig, then began to enjoy the attention as Elaine tore one of her underskirts free and began to wrap his arm. Soon the bleeding was stopped.

She looked up and said, "Now, that's better."

King Dion came to stand by the young man. "My boy," he said, "you have saved the lives of the king, the queen, and the royal princess!" He looked at Sir Gwin. "Let me have your sword."

The knight handed it to him, and the king said, "Kneel, Reb Jackson."

Without understanding what was happening, Reb struggled to his knees. He felt the touch of the sword on his shoulder, and he heard the king say, "Arise, Sir Reb!"

8

A Message from the Dark Lord

Elmas, the Chief Interrogator of the Sanhedrin, feared few people. He was so accustomed to having his word obeyed and to seeing fear come into the eyes of his servants that it always came as a shock whenever he himself felt fear. And that terrible fear came whenever the Dark Lord summoned him.

Now, arrayed in his crimson robe, a gold chain around his neck, a medallion bearing a strange device bumping against his chest, he entered the chamber of the Dark Lord. He found that his breath was coming faster and that his stomach began to tighten. When he was inside, he fell on his knees before the powerful being that sat in the darkness of a throne.

"I am come, my Lord."

The Dark Lord gave him one swift look, and his lips curled. His eyes were fathomless depths of evil. There was, indeed, an aura of evil that hung like a cloud about this powerful commander of an empire.

"You have failed me again, Elmas," the Dark Lord said, his voice ringing like a hollow bell in the chamber. "If you cannot fulfill your functions, I have others who can."

Elmas began to tremble. He cupped his hands together and raised them. "Oh, my lord, do not speak so. You must know that I have always obeyed your commands."

"Obedience is not enough," the Dark Lord snapped. He rose from his throne, tall, dark, somber, wearing a black robe with a hood that shielded most of his features. Only the red gleam of his eyes and the cruel lips were visible. "I have commissioned you twice for a mission concerning these accursed Sleepers. Both times you have failed me."

"It was not my fault." Elmas's teeth chattered. "Goel aided them—"

"*Goel!* You know I have forbidden anyone to utter that name!" The Dark Lord moved close, reached down, and caught the quaking priest by the throat. He jerked him up, almost spitting out the name. "*'Goel.* The house of Goel will be filled.'" He shook Elmas as a terrier shakes a rat. "Next you will be joining this uprising that is trying to bring Goel and his pitiful servants to rule in Nuworld." He glanced callously at the swollen face of Elmas, then shoved him away.

Elmas fell backward, clawing at his throat. The sucking in of his breath made a painful noise. Nevertheless, he scrambled to his feet and held up his hands again. "I will not fail you this time, Sire."

"Very well," the Dark Lord said in a deadly voice, "You have one more opportunity. See that you do not fail. What is the situation?"

"I will send a messenger at once," Elmas said quickly. He was breathing a little easier now. "We have one of ours in Camelot. He is a clever and ruthless man. I will at once alert him to the danger of the Sleepers."

"Get out. See that it is done."

The Dark Lord watched the priest scramble out of the chamber. "Fool," he said. He struck the wall with his fist, and it seemed that the rocks trembled with his power. "Always these Sleepers! Always Goel!" He clenched his fist again, and the evil in his face grew more pronounced. "I will pull the flesh off their bones, all of them! They will not take my kingdom!"

* * *

"Sire, a messenger has just arrived." The servant who had come to the chamber of Lord Melchior watched apprehensively. One never knew how Melchior would take things. "He says that it is urgent."

Melchior gave the servant a sour glance. "Who is he? What is his name?"

"He will not give his name—but he says he comes from Elmas, of the Sanhedrin."

Melchior glanced up, his eyes flickering with interest. "Sanhedrin, eh? Well, show him in."

When the servant had left, Melchior reached out and poured a stream of red wine into a silver flagon. He lifted it to his lips, sipped, and murmured to himself, "So. The Sanhedrin now is sending messages. I know Elmas. He'll use me if he can—but two can play at that game!"

The door swung open, and a small man dressed in a green cloak, shabby and worn, entered. A hood covered his head, and he bowed slightly. "Sir Melchior, I have a message from Elmas, my master."

"Well, what is the message? Give it to me."

"It is not written down, Sire. Such things would be too dangerous." The messenger threw his cloak back, and Melchior blinked at the features of the man who stood before him. He was an albino—his eyebrows and hair were colorless and even his eyes a milky white. "My master commands me to tell you that it is urgent that you capture those who have come to Camelot."

"'Those who have come'?" Melchior questioned. "Many people have come to Camelot."

A sullen expression came into the messenger's face. "Not like these. They are the most dangerous opponents of our kingdom."

"I have heard of no newcomers of such importance. Surely I would have heard if such emissaries had come."

"Not necessarily, Sir Melchior." The messenger shook his head. "These are very deceitful messengers. They are all very young, none over fifteen."

"Children!" Melchior snorted in amazement. "I am to capture *children?* Has it come to that?"

"Do not take the matter so lightly! These are the servants of Goel. Their power we can only guess at, but they have escaped traps and have foiled the intentions and plans of the Dark Lord. It is he, my master says, who commands that the Seven Sleepers be captured or killed."

Melchior stared at him, then said, "Sit down. I'll have food brought."

When the messenger had seated himself, Melchior poured a flagon of wine and shoved it before him. As the man drank thirstily, Melchior said, "Now, tell me all you know about the 'Seven Sleepers.'"

* * *

The entire castle of Camelot was decorated with banners of red and blue and yellow—the colors of King Dion. The smell of roasted meat and fresh bread was in the air in front of the jousting field. The stands were filled with the nobility of the kingdom. Out on the far side of the field the groundlings watched as knights practiced their swordplay, fencing with one another while the grooms kept the horses ready for the activities.

"This will be your first tournament," Elaine said to Reb. Her smile was sweet and gentle. "I hope it will not be your last."

Reb shot her a surprised look. "You mean I might get kilt?"

A worried look crossed the princess's face. "It's not unknown. These tournaments are very dangerous. Some think they shouldn't even be held." She shook her head. "I am worried about you, Reb."

His pride touched, Reb said, "Why, shoot, don't worry about me, Miss Elaine! I'll be all right."

The princess looked on him fondly. "I'll hope for that." She gazed across the field. "Look, the knights are getting ready for the melee."

"The melee? What's that?"

"Well, it's actually a mock battle. You see down there —those are the red knights. They represent the king. And there, down the other side"—Reb looked to where she was pointing and saw a group of knights dressed in black—"those are the black knights."

"Well, what are they going to do?"

"As I said, they are going to have a pretend sword battle. You see, they are lining up, and when my father gives the signal they will charge down the field toward each other."

Reb saw that the knights had drawn their swords. All were clad in full armor. "It does look pretty dangerous, doesn't it?"

"Yes. See, there is Loren, my brother, at the head of the red knights. This is his second tournament. He did very well last year." She looked down at the knights dressed in black. "These are the best knights of the kingdom. Do you see the man in front on the big black horse?"

"Yep. He's not as big as a horse—but he ain't much littler either!"

"His name is Sir Melchior." A troubled look came into Elaine's eyes. "He's a troublesome man. My father says he's very ambitious."

"Well, he's a big one."

Reb was impressed with the chief of the black forces. Melchior was dressed from head to foot in gleaming armor, but over it he wore black. His helmet had a black ostrich plume, and he clasped a long sword that caught the gleam of the sunlight.

At that moment a rider came out and announced, "Now, all will bear witness that honor must be maintained. Any man who falls from his horse must not be attacked. The king has commanded that mercy be shown the wounded." The herald continued to give the regulations of the melee, then rode back to where King Dion sat on a platform.

The king looked fondly at his son, then at the black forces, and raised his scepter. All the horsemen held their reins tightly, ready for the signal. Then King Dion lowered the scepter, and the two forces, with a loud shout, began to gallop toward each other.

Reb's eyes were wide as he watched. He blinked when the opposing riders came together with a crash. He saw Prince Loren parry a blow and knock one knight to the ground with a skillful thrust of his sword. The air was filled with the clanging of steel blades against blades, of the cry of pain as men were driven from their saddles, and the crash of armor as they fell to the ground.

"Look! Melchior's going to strike that man who fell!" Elaine cried.

Melchior, indeed, had knocked from his horse one of the chieftains wearing the colors of King Dion, and he raised his sword to strike the helpless man.

Then a trumpet sounded. Melchior glanced up swiftly and saw the king glaring at him. He spoke to the wounded man. "Leave the arena." Then he turned to enter the battle again.

The melee went on for a long time. Man after man fell to the ground and limped off the field. The stable men came and led away their horses, some of them wounded as well.

Finally, when the two sides had almost the same number of survivors, the king stood. "Enough! I declare a tie."

Both Melchior and Prince Loren began to protest.

"Let us finish the melee," the prince said.

"No, we have had enough. You have proved your courage, my son. You and all of the men."

Melchior raised his visor. His eyes were hot with battle as he rode up to the platform where King Dion and the queen were sitting.

"Your Majesty," he said, "you are wise to call off the melee." He smiled, and his white teeth gleamed against his dark skin. He was not a man without charm, this Melchior, and he knew how to draw men to him and how to hold them. He was a strong man as well, in every way, and now he said, "Sire, let us have one more contest. That will settle the winner of the tournament."

A mutter ran around, and Loren said, "Yes, you and me, Sir Melchior, in a joust."

The two had jousted before, with Loren losing twice to the older, stronger man. He seemed anxious to redeem himself, but Melchior shook his head. "We are your guests, Your Majesty, and since the melee has been inconclusive, as a guest I ask you to put forth a man to joust with me, and I ask you also to let me choose that man."

King Dion stared at the tall form cloaked in black. The king was not a man to know fear—but if he were, this was the man he would have feared. He knew Melchior had gathered to himself discontented men, knights who had grudges against the crown and against the kingdom. He knew that daily Melchior's power grew. The king was suspicious, and yet he could sense the crowd's approval.

"Very well, let it be so. Who do you choose as your opponent—Sir Gwin, perhaps?"

"Sir Gwin is an opponent worthy of my steel," Sir Melchior said. "But no." Then he looked to the king's right where the Seven Sleepers sat on a somewhat lower platform. "I have heard of your guests the Seven Sleepers. I have especially heard of the one called 'Reb,' now 'Sir Reb.'"

Reb had been sitting loosely, watching the encounter with fascination, but now, as he saw the hard eyes of Sir Melchior fixed on him, he swallowed, and his face grew red. Everyone in the arena had turned to look at him, and he muttered, "How'd he hear about me, Princess?"

"I don't know, but whatever he says, don't have anything to do with him. He's evil!" she whispered, her voice tense.

Sir Melchior moved his horse, using only his knees. The huge stallion came to the front of the box where the Sleepers were sitting, and Melchior looked them over carefully. There was something sinister in the way he studied them.

Josh's hand went to his sword instinctively. "He's up to something, Sarah," he muttered. "I don't like the looks of it."

Melchior held Reb's gaze for one moment, then looked at the king. "Would it not be fitting that your champion should be one whom you have just chosen for his bravery?"

"He's but a boy!" King Dion protested.

"I understand that he is a little more than that," Sir Melchior stated flatly. "He has unhorsed some of your best knights, has he not?"

"Well, that's true but—"

"And I understand his courage is unquestioned since he saved your life by facing a wild boar. Have I heard correctly, Your Majesty?"

"The boy is brave and a fine jouster—but I would not have him risk himself against a man such as yourself."

Melchior turned and looked at the Seven Sleepers. He smiled. "You are not a coward, I trust, Sir Reb?"

Reb stood to his feet, overcome with anger. "I'll fight

you," he said. As soon as he had spoken, he knew that he had made a mistake.

Josh's fierce whisper came, "Sit down, you fool. You can't fight a man like that!"

But Sir Melchior had heard Reb's response. He turned to the king. "Now, there's a man with spirit! I like to see young men who take their honor seriously. When shall we have the contest, Your Majesty?"

King Dion sought for a way to pull back. Somehow he knew this was going to be a disaster—but his honor was at stake, and the young man had accepted the challenge. Now he had no choice.

"The joust between Sir Melchior and Sir Reb will take place at noon tomorrow."

The king then dismissed the crowd, and the Sleepers swarmed around Reb. All begged him to change his mind.

Elaine was with them. She stood beside him, her eyes pleading. "Reb, you don't know what a cruel man Sir Melchior is. For some reason he hates you. I could see it."

"Shore, I could see it too," Reb said slowly. "He hates all of us for some reason."

Josh said suddenly, "I wonder if he could be in the service of the Dark Lord?"

His words brought a silence over the group.

Finally Reb said, "Well, Dark Lord or not, I'm going to stop his clock! We'll just see if he can put his money where his mouth is!" His words were bold, but inside he was beginning to feel a little queasy.

When the young men got back to their quarters, Josh and Dave tried to talk Reb into putting off the tournament. "Wait a week or two," Dave said. "You could get in some more practice, learn more about his style."

Josh agreed. "Yes, no one will think anything about that. After all, you're an amateur practically, and he's a professional."

But Reb's pride had been stirred. He shook his head, his jaw set grimly. "No, I'm going to fight that beast tomorrow or know the reason why!"

Josh gave the boy a careful look and shook his head. "Someday, Reb, you're going to learn that sometimes wisdom is better than throwing yourself into a fight."

9

The Revenge of Melchior

The news of the contest between the young stranger Sir Reb and the mighty warrior Sir Melchior spread like wildfire. Long before noon the fields were crowded, and every knight and noble had packed himself into the stands. The gossip was that if Sir Melchior won the battle he would somehow make things hard for the king.

"It's gotten to be kind of a symbol," Josh said in a puzzled tone. He was standing off to one side with Sarah and the others as the three foremost knights in King Dion's service clustered around Reb, giving him advice.

"I don't know about a symbol," she said, "but somehow this joust has become more important than it should be." She glanced toward Reb, who was looking from one knight to another, a confused expression spreading over his features. "Isn't there something we can do to talk him out of it?"

Wash shook his head. "You know what he says about himself. He says he's stubborn as a bluenose mule—whatever that is. I tried all night to get him to change his mind. He just flat won't do it."

Abigail looked with apprehension down the field to where Sir Melchior was joking with one of his lieutenants. "It's just not fair," she said, and then a light came into her eyes. "But wouldn't it be wonderful if Sir Reb beat that big bully?"

"Not much chance of that, Abbey." Dave grunted. "From what I hear he's *numero uno* when it comes to jousting. I talked to Sir Gwin about him. Gwin says he wasn't sure that even *he* could give him a tumble."

* * *

Sir Gwin was saying something like that to Reb at that very moment.

"Now, my boy, it's not too late to back off." He had grown to like and admire the young man, one of the finest horsemen he had ever seen and full of courage as well. "After all, it's not really right, don't you know?"

Reb was pale, so much so that his freckles stood out. He had seen men maimed in jousts much less serious than this one. But he only shook his head stubbornly. "I'm gonna do it, Sir Gwin, and that's all there is to it."

Sir Elbert's large, round face was gloomy. "You'd best fall off as soon as his lance touches you, my boy. No sense getting killed in a lost cause." Sir Elbert always took the pessimistic view of things. Looking at Sir Melchior, he measured the knight and said, "You're too young to die, my boy. Better just fall off your horse."

Sir Nolen knew Reb the best. This small, muscular man was the best horseman in King Dion's court. "Here, you two stop pestering the lad!" he snapped. He put his hand on Reb's shoulder, having to reach up to do it. "I always say, a good horse is half the joust. Right?"

"That's right." Reb grinned suddenly. "And Thunder here is as good a horse as that old Melchior's likely to have."

"Well, his is larger," Sir Nolen said, "but he is slower too and won't respond as quick. Now, have you got your mind made up as to how to fight him?"

"Well," Reb said slowly, "he's bigger than I am, got more weight, so if he hits me square, he'll knock me off the horse. That's all there is to it. Somehow, I've got to make him miss."

Gwin nodded eagerly. "You could try the trick you used before. Aim for the head—that'll bring his lance up and make him duck. Then smack him right in the belly."

Reb looked across the field, thinking hard. "I don't think he's stupid, Sir Gwin. I'll bet he's heard all about that. I'll bet he'll be looking for exactly that kind of trick, and if I try it he'll nail me sure."

Sir Gwin scratched his head. "You may be right about that." He looked puzzled, then defeated. "Well, I don't know what to say, my boy. Just trust your good right arm and your horse. That's all a man can do anyway."

"No, it's not." Reb had a sudden thought that reflected in his eyes. His lips grew tight. "Somehow, in a mess like this, I always know that Goel is watching. You wouldn't believe how many awful predicaments he's gotten my friends and me out of. So I guess he'll just have to do it again."

"But he's not here," Sir Elbert protested.

"That don't seem to matter. He seems to be able to take care of things even when he's not around."

A silver, snarling trumpet began to chide the afternoon air.

Sir Gwin said, "All right. Time to go. Come along. We'll put you on your horse."

They moved to where the horses were waiting, and, as always, Reb was a little shocked at how an armed knight got on a horse. He was accustomed to just stepping into the stirrup and throwing his other leg across. But weighed down with armor, that would be very difficult! So a hoist of sorts had been constructed.

Now a rope was slid under his arms, and he was lifted in the air. Then Thunder was led under him by the groom. When he was lowered into the saddle, he looked down and shook his head. "Sir Gwin, I never thought I'd have to get hoisted on a horse."

"The best of us do it, my boy." Sir Gwin tried to smile. "Now, here's your lance." He handed Reb the wooden spear.

At the same time Sir Nolen came with his shield. "Here you are, Sir Reb." He watched as the boy secured the shield to his left arm. "Remember, you've got the best horse, and you've got the best cause."

"You're right about that, Nolen," Sir Gwin said. His jaw tightened. "I wish I were riding against that villain. I'd like to see him tumbled in the dirt!" He looked back to Reb and said, "Give it the best you've got."

"You can bet on it!" Reb muttered. Guiding Thunder with his knees, he guided the strong animal to the south end of the tilting field, turned him around, and marveled at the horse's obedience.

Lifting his eyes, he saw the black horse of Sir Melchior and then the man himself. A flash of sunlight touched the dark knight's visor, and Reb murmured, "Well, if Goel don't help me, I'm sure in a mess."

He had been over and over that matter all night long. It was true that the men of Camelot were small, smaller than the average men of Oldworld. He himself was taller than most of them—was as tall as Melchior for that matter. But Melchior was thick and strong and had years of training. He could do this sort of thing in his sleep.

A worried frown crossed Reb's face as he pulled down his visor. Now he could see only through the slits in the armor, but he heard the words of the warden announcing the battle and the rules that governed it. Reb paid no attention to this. He had heard it before. Sir Melchior, he knew, would probably smash him from his horse with all the force he could muster.

"How can I do it?" he muttered desperately. "I can't let everybody down. They're all expecting me to do something to pull this thing out." Then, as the warden's voice fell away, he waited for the signal, another blast on the trumpet. "Got to think of something!" he said desperately.

And just as the trumpet sounded, a thought came to him. He did not have time to analyze it. Only for one blinding moment did the idea flash into his head. But in that instant he knew exactly what he could do—and he realized that the thought had come from Goel!

At the trumpet blast Thunder lunged forward. Down the field Sir Melchior leaned over his saddle, making himself a smaller target, his lance leveled.

It was for that brief time as though everything else had faded away. Reb could not hear the cheering crowd or the crying trumpets as he raced toward his opponent. All he heard was the sound of Thunder's hooves and the creaking of his armor, and all he saw was Sir Melchior. It was as if he were looking through a tunnel, and there, facing him, eyes blazing through his visor, Melchior seemed to be laughing at him.

Reb suddenly felt that the whole world had stopped and that he and Melchior alone were moving, and slowly at that. The horses were galloping, galloping, closing the distance, but all seemed to be happening very, very slowly. He was now close enough to see the fine scrollwork on Melchior's armor. He saw also the tip of the lance that was aimed directly at him.

"No time," he gasped. "This will *have* to work!" Shutting out all thoughts of failure, he got ready to perform a movement that he never would have dreamed of and that no one in the arena had ever seen.

The point of jousting, he knew, was to put the tip of your lance into the shield of your opponent—before he put the tip of his lance into yours. Theoretically, if one man had a ten-foot lance and one man had a twelve-foot lance, the man with the longer lance would win the joust because his lance would arrive a split second sooner. However, the art of jousting had evolved to such an extent that all lances were practically the same length.

Reb had already decided that he would have no chance whatsoever in a head-on crash, even if his lance reached the shield of Sir Melchior at the same instant that Sir Melchior's touched him. He knew that the heavier weight and skill of the older man would topple him. So he did what had come to him in his brief, flashing thought.

A split second before Sir Melchior threw himself forward—a shout in his throat and victory in his eye, with his lance piercing the air, headed straight for Reb's shield—Reb touched Thunder with his left knee.

Now jousting horses knew to keep straight on the track, but at Reb's touch the fiery stallion abruptly swerved to the right.

Melchior was not prepared for that—nor was he prepared for what Reb did next. At the same instant Thunder veered right, Reb moved his lance across his body—pointing directly to the left. The point was not aimed at Sir Melchior's shield or head at all.

What happened then was almost inevitable. Reb felt Melchior's lance graze his arm. Six inches farther and he would have been knocked off the horse. A split second later, as Reb braced himself, Sir Melchior ran into the lance Reb held in his path. It caught him right under the chin, and the force of his horse and the force of the blow worked together. Sir Melchior pitched backward and hit the ground with a clanging clash. His horse ran wildly on.

Thunder did the same.

As soon as Reb could get control of his horse, he whirled around. And now heard the screaming crowd.

"Why, I've never seen anything like it!" King Dion cried. "My, what a victory!"

As soon as the crowd saw the king's approval, they went wild.

Reb found himself surrounded by a cheering throng. His horse was led to the stand, and every hand wanted to reach up and pat him or Thunder.

Finally, he stood before the king.

King Dion rose to his feet, a smile wreathing his face. "Sir Reb," he said, "I have already knighted you, and I cannot do that again. I must then express my gratitude to you for upholding the honor of the court in such splendid fashion."

Reb had pulled off his helmet. Now he handed it down to Josh, who took it, a grin spreading across his face.

"Aw, shucks, Your Majesty, I'm glad I was able to do so good, but it wasn't me."

"It wasn't *you?*" King Dion's face had a puzzled expression. "Of course it was you!"

"No, not really," Reb said. He looked across at Elendar, who was smiling and whose eyes burned with a joy Reb had not seen. "Actually what happened was the power of Goel. He's the one that should get the glory for this, not me."

A cheer went up from the Seven Sleepers. "To Goel! To Goel!" they all cried out.

And then the crowd took it up: "To Goel! To Goel!"

As Reb slipped from his horse, Elaine was there, and she pulled his head down to whisper, "I'm so very proud of you, Reb."

Reb had learned a little of chivalry toward ladies and had sense enough to reach down and take her hand and kiss it. "Well, Princess, if you're happy, I'm happy."

He was pulled away, but before he left, she said, "Reb, next time I wish you would wear my favor on your lance."

Reb's lips broke into a grin. "You can believe that,

Princess." Then he was led away to be the chief guest at the celebration.

* * *

He did not look back, but if he had, he would have seen Melchior glaring at him with hate-filled eyes. And had he been close enough, he would have heard Melchior say to his lieutenant, Sir Baloc, "All right, they won this round, but there's another one to play."

* * *

The boys awoke when a terrible banging sounded in their room. Josh was the first one out of bed. "Something must be wrong!" He opened the door and was amazed to see Prince Loren.

The prince's eyes were wild, and his hair was mussed. "Come," he said, "there's an emergency meeting."

"What is it?" Josh cried out as he scrambled for his clothes. "Is there a war?"

Loren gave him a hard look, and his lips were a thin white line. "There's probably going to be one before this is over."

Josh pulled his boots on, then rose to his feet.

Reb was beside him. "What is it, Prince Loren?"

Loren's eyes were fixed on Reb. "You did a good thing putting Melchior down, but I think he's found a way to get some revenge on all of us."

Reb stared. "What do you mean?"

Loren ground his teeth and slapped his fist angrily into his palm. "He's kidnapped my sister."

"Elaine?" Josh cried out in alarm. "Why, that can't be."

"But it is," Loren said grimly. "Come now, the war council is meeting. The king commands your presence there."

The five boys hurried with Prince Loren down the corridor. On the way they were joined by Abigail and Sarah, both white-faced with anxiety.

"What will it mean, Josh?" Sarah whispered.

"Like Loren says, it'll mean war," Josh said grimly. "The king will never allow his daughter to be kidnapped."

Sarah nodded slowly. "Oh, I wish Goel were here to get her back."

Josh thought about that. "You know Goel doesn't do things much by himself." He looked over at the others. "He usually has someone do what he wants done for him—and this time, it's gonna be a real chore!"

10

The Winner of the Quest

The news of the abduction of Princess Elaine stirred the Kingdom of Camelot into fierce activity. Sir Gwin, in charge of the battle forces, summoned all his lieutenants. They, in turn, rode at once to procure their followers.

King Dion and the queen were distraught.

While they waited in their quarters for word to come from Sir Gwin, Queen Mauve went to the window and looked down on the court. She saw the stir below, knights readying their armament, stablemen grooming their horses, and everywhere people whispering and buzzing in small groups. She turned away from the scene and said, "What will come of all this? How could he *do* it?"

King Dion looked older than his years. His dark blue eyes were weary, for he had been up all night talking with his council, and his shoulders were stooped. "He did it very cleverly. Actually, we have no word from Melchior. It's his lieutenant, Sir Baloc, who's done the thing."

A shiver went over the queen's shoulders. She clasped her hands and closed her eyes. "Baloc! I hate that man! He's so cruel." She stood before the king, who was slumped in a chair. "But how could he hope to get away with it? He must know that it will mean war."

"I don't know, but I suspect that he'll take refuge with Melchior. Then Melchior will expect us to come in and begin hostilities, and then he'll have his excuse to attack."

"But he can't be that powerful, can he? I mean . . ." The queen hesitated. "He can't defeat our army, can he, dear?"

Dion sighed heavily, then got to his feet and took her hands. "I honestly don't know. A few years ago, I would have said no, but something has been happening to our kingdom. It's like a . . . a shadow is falling over it! It gets darker almost every day."

Mauve stared up at him. "Do you think it's the Dark Lord?"

"Elendar thinks so. He tried to get me to take action years ago, but I was a fool and wouldn't listen to him. And now it's a question of whether we'll be strong enough to stand against Melchior's powers. I wish—"

A knock sounded at the door, and Queen Mauve said, "Come in."

Sir Gwin marched in, an excited, serious look on his face. "We have a message, Your Majesty, from Sir Baloc."

The king and queen exchanged hurried glances. Then King Dion said, "What is the message?"

Sir Gwin slapped his hands together. "So arrogant! I'd like to get that fellow between my two hands. I'd squeeze his throat until his eyeballs popped."

"Yes, yes, but what about the message? What about Elaine?" Queen Mauve demanded. "Is she all right?"

"For now, she is." Sir Gwin nodded. "But that fellow Baloc, he's demanding that you give your permission for him to marry Elaine."

"What!" King Dion straightened up, and fire leaped into his eyes. His hand went to where his sword should be, but he wasn't wearing it. "Why, the man's insane!"

Queen Mauve asked, "What exactly was the message, Sir Gwin?"

"Oh, it was as arrogant as the man himself. He offered himself as a husband and made it plain that he felt you couldn't get a better son-in-law."

"What are we going to do?" Mauve asked, putting her hand on her husband's arm. "Surely, he can't mean it."

"He probably does," Dion said grimly. "It would be like giving Melchior a key to the castle gates. His lieutenant comes in as our son-in-law, and—once he's inside—his evil influence can work throughout all our guards, all our knights. The first thing you know, he's perverted them, and they're ready to go over to Melchior's side." He beat his hand against the wall. "Then the Dark Lord would have it all."

Sir Gwin hesitated, then said, "He did add one more thing to his 'offer.'"

"And what was that?"

"He said that he will not set Elaine free until a challenger comes. That's what he would like. We send a challenger over, he tricks him—whoever it is—claims the victory, and then claims Princess Elaine."

"Just the sort of thing he would do. The trouble is," King Dion said slowly, "I'm not sure we're strong enough to go to war."

"You're right there, Your Majesty. It would be a close thing. We might win, but the dead would be a mighty list of our best men."

Queen Mauve was staring at her husband. Finally she asked, "Are you thinking of sending a challenger, dear?"

King Dion's eyes were half shut. He was past his youth, but his mind was as keen as ever. "Yes," he said suddenly, "I think we must."

"But what if the challenger is defeated?"

"If he is, then we go after her with everything we've got," the king answered grimly. "But there's just one chance in a thousand that somehow we'll be able to do this through the quest and the challenge."

"Let *me* go, Your Majesty," Sir Gwin exclaimed. "I would be honored to take the task upon myself."

With a fond glance at his lieutenant the king slowly shook his head. "Not this time, Sir Gwin. Let it be known that the challenger who will take up Baloc's challenge will be chosen by lot. Every knight who wishes will have an opportunity."

"Is that wise, Sire?" Sir Gwin asked, a worried frown on his face. "After all, in a situation like that, the name of one of our knights of lesser ability might be drawn."

"I'm sure only the more able knights will volunteer. But more important—I'm not much of a believer in impulses, but this thought has come to me very strongly." He stroked his beard and looked down at the floor for a long moment. Finally he lifted his eyes. "I believe this idea was *given* to me somehow. I certainly would never have thought of it myself."

Queen Mauve asked, "Do you think it might be some sort of message from Goel?"

"I'm not sure, but the thought came to me so strongly that I feel we must try it." He turned to Sir Gwin. "Call the council together. They will argue, but I will carry them. You will at once prepare to carry out the name drawing. It must be open and aboveboard—no trickery."

"Certainly not, Your Majesty," Sir Gwin said rather indignantly. "I myself will see to the integrity of it all."

As soon as he was gone, King Dion put his arms around his wife. "I'm not at all sure about this. Things seem so confused."

"Yes, I know, dear." She reached up and stroked his cheek. "I wish we were back in those days when the Dark Lord had no hold on our kingdom."

King Dion straightened himself to his full height. "We will see those days again. I feel it in my bones!"

* * *

"Well, all the knights in the kingdom who want to have put their names in the lottery," Josh said. "Have you talked to the king about this, Elendar?"

"Yes." The old man was staring out a window.

He had sent for Josh, and the two talked long about the significance of Elaine's abduction. Elendar had said at once, "It's the first move on Melchior's part to break the Sword of Camelot and bring the realm under his control."

Now he turned to look Josh in the eye. "I've talked to the king about it. He's very stubborn, more stubborn than I've ever seen him. He says that this thing didn't come from his own heart, that it just—flashed into his mind. That's the way he put it."

"What do you think, Elendar?"

"I think he may be right. Open war would be disastrous right now. Until we can build up our forces, I'm not ready to meet Melchior in all-out warfare. This scheme— if it is of Goel—will be better than that."

"Well," Josh said, "I think we'd better be getting over to the arena for the name drawing. It's almost noon."

"Yes, and I don't mind admitting I'm a little bit nervous about the whole thing."

They made their way from the upper story of the castle, down a winding set of stairs, then outside, and walked to the open field. It was filled with people.

"It looks like they're ready to draw the name," Elendar said quietly. "Come, let's stand closer."

Because of his authority, Elendar pressed through the crowd. People gave way before him, most of them bowing, and Josh stayed close by his side. Soon they were right below the platform where the king and queen were seated.

Sir Gwin stood before a large oak box. He looked very nervous and kept stroking his mustache with a hand that was not quite steady.

"Sound the trumpet," the king commanded, and the brazen voice of the instrument smote the air.

"Hear ye! Hear ye! His Majesty, King Dion of Camelot, will now address his subjects."

King Dion rose, bowed to Queen Mauve, then faced the crowd. "My loving subjects," he said rather quietly, but his voice carried over the large field, "I need not tell you of the crisis that has come upon us. You are all aware that our daughter is being held captive. You are also aware that, unless a challenger goes forth to meet Sir Baloc, we will be forced to go to war."

He hesitated. Then his eyes met those of Elendar, and the hoary head of the old man nodded slightly in encouragement. This seemed to help the king, and he raised his voice. "I believe I have been given direction to hold a drawing to select the knight who is to challenge Melchior. Every volunteer has put his name on a slip of paper. Those slips have been in this box and have been guarded by my chief of knights, Sir Gwin. We are now ready to draw that name."

The king moved down to the box, stood over it, and said, "I, myself, will draw the name so that there will be no charge of favoritism or of dishonesty."

A hush fell over the crowd, and Josh stared at the king as he bent over the box. He hesitated after reaching into the chest, as though he were sorting through the pieces of paper. Then he drew out a slip and looked at it.

What he saw seemed to turn the king to stone, for he did not move a muscle. A light wind blew his white hair about his neck beneath the crown, as every ear in the crowd strained to hear the name he would read.

King Dion looked up, his eyes searching the throng. "The knight who has been chosen is . . ."

Everyone seemed to lean forward on tiptoe, waiting.

And then King Dion turned to look straight at the Seven Sleepers. "The knight who is chosen is Sir Reb."

A gasp went up. Several knights frowned and began to grumble, but King Dion looked at them sternly, and they grew silent. The king said, "Sir Reb, come forward."

Reb was the most surprised person in the arena. His mind was almost a blank. He could not believe this. He had put his name on a slip of paper, but never once had it occurred to him that he might be chosen. Coming to stand before the king, he saw something in the king's expression that he could not define.

King Dion said, "Are you ready to assume this quest, Sir Reb?"

And then, Bob Lee Jackson stood straight and tall. "Yes, Your Majesty. I don't stake no claim to being the strongest or the best—but you can bet I'll do all I can to save Princess Elaine!"

11

The Scent of Death

The morning sun lighted the eastern sky as the two horsemen paused to look back down into the valley. Camelot gleamed like old gold, and Wash gave it a wistful look. "I sure wish we was taking the whole army with us," he said.

Reb shook his head. "Aw, Wash, we don't need an army. We'll do all right."

They had left the city just before dawn, after being roused from sleep by Elendar.

The old man took them to where their horses were saddled and said to Reb, "Every knight needs a squire, and I am sending one with you that I have great confidence in." He smiled fondly on the small, black boy, laid a hand on his shoulder, and said, "My son, you have one quality that Sir Reb lacks—and that is caution." Then he looked intently at Reb. "You are going on a task I cannot help you with. Trust Goel. Listen to the words of wisdom that come from your squire."

Reb paused as he was about to mount Thunder. "Are you telling me that I'm going to fail, Elendar? Is that it?"

Elendar shook his head. "I am no soothsayer. I cannot tell what will happen in the future, except at times a dark cloud seems to lie over it. When that happens I know who is at hand."

"You mean the Dark Lord," Wash said. He drew his cloak close around him and shivered a little. "I don't want to meet up with that cat!" He glanced at Elendar. "Are you *sure* that I'm the one you want to go with Reb?"

"Yes, I'm certain about that." He gave Reb a worried frown. "I'm sure about little else, though. But it seems that Goel has put you in this place. Sometimes," he said thoughtfully, "difficult circumstances test us. Princess Elaine must be rescued, the kingdom must be saved—but I think all this has happened to bring you to a place of testing —and learning." He suddenly appeared tired, and he waved a hand. "Go now, and remember to listen for the words of Goel. They come at the most unexpected times."

"We will, Elendar. Don't you fret." Reb sprang into his saddle as Wash laboriously climbed onto his small pony and took the lines of the packhorse that carried Reb's armor and their camping gear. "I'll be careful," he said cheerfully.

Now as they looked down upon Camelot, Reb mused, "Well, Wash, when you first woke up in that capsule, I bet you never thought you'd be going on an adventure like this."

"No, I didn't," Wash agreed. "Reminds me of what President Abraham Lincoln said once when somebody complimented him on being elected president."

"What was that?"

"Mr. Lincoln said he felt like the man that was tarred and feathered and ridden out of town on a rail. He said, 'If it wasn't for the honor of the thing, why, I'd just as soon walk.'"

Reb laughed heartily. "Come on, let's ramble. According to the map Sir Gwin gave us, we've got a long day's ride."

The two rode hard all morning, paused at noon for a brief meal, then for the rest of the afternoon made their way across mountain ridges, through forests, and across plains. When nightfall came, they camped beside a small stream.

Wash was the better cook. So Reb gathered firewood as Wash unpacked the supplies. Soon they were eating and watching the fire flicker in the darkness. A quietness was upon the land, but it seemed an uneasy sort of silence.

"I don't like this country," Wash said, drawing his cloak closer about him. He bit down on a piece of roasted meat skewered on a stick, chewed thoughtfully, and gazed out into the blackness. "There's something spooky about this place."

Reb was looking at the map, planning their next day's journey. "Well, it's called 'Darkwood.' I guess that's spooky enough. But don't worry. We'll be out of it in the morning—according to this map."

"I wish it was now, Reb. I got a funny feeling about this place."

Neither boy wanted to go to sleep. There *was* something sinister about Darkwood. The trees overhead seemed to be whispering. And it wasn't just noise, Wash thought; it was as if they were speaking to one another. Far off, the wind howled as it cut through a mountain pass—a lonesome, mournful, and even threatening sound.

Before long, though, they both grew sleepy. Reb was pulling out his blanket when suddenly Wash jumped up. "Reb," he cried, "there's somebody out there!"

At once Reb drew his sword and leaped to his feet. Straining his eyes, he stared into the darkness. "Who's there?" he called loudly. "Who are you?"

A figure advanced, and as Reb and Wash stood poised, ready for anything, a voice said, "I come in peace."

Wash stared in amazement, for he had expected to see an enemy, a man of war. Instead, the one who stepped into the light of their small campfire appeared to be a rather small girl wearing a long, dark green cloak. But when she threw back the hood, her black hair cascaded around her

103

shoulders and a full-grown woman was revealed. She was very beautiful.

Wash was still suspicious. "Who are you, and what are you doing coming at us in the middle of the night?"

"I don't blame you for being suspicious," the young woman said. She appeared to be no more than seventeen or eighteen, and her eyes were as dark as her hair. "My name is Mogen, and you are Sir Reb." She curtsied. "And this is your squire, Wash." She fastened her eyes on the smaller boy and smiled. "I have no weapon as you see, and, as I said, I come in peace."

Feeling a little foolish, the boys sheathed their swords.

Wash said, "How come you know all about us?"

"Why, everyone knows about the quest," the young woman said. "All of Camelot has its eyes fixed upon you, Sir Reb."

Her words seemed to please Reb. "Well, that may just be. But I guess somebody's got to do it." He glanced into the darkness and back at the girl. "But what are you doing out here in the middle of nowhere?"

"I have traveled far," Mogen said, "and am very tired. Perhaps you will share your meal with me."

"Why, shore." Reb nodded. "Wash, let's see if we can pull together something for this lady."

The two busied themselves, and Mogen sat down, watching them with her dark eyes. They put food before her, and she ate and drank some of the juice they had brought in leather skins. "Thank you," she said finally. "I have come a long way."

"A long way from where?" Wash insisted. He gave Reb a sharp look. "I don't want to seem unfriendly, but we don't know you."

Mogen looked into his face and smiled slightly. "Sir Reb has a good counselor. It is well not to put too much trust in strangers until they prove themselves." Then she fastened her eyes on Reb. "But I think you will welcome me when you find out my mission. Goel has sent me to you."

"Goel!" Reb shot a sharp look at Wash, and his mouth fell open. "Wow!" he exclaimed. "I'm glad to hear that!"

"I thought you might be." Mogen nodded. "On a dangerous mission such as yours, a man needs a word from Goel."

Wash was looking at her carefully. He could hear, faintly, the moan of the wind rising in the hills, and again the trees seemed to whisper overhead.

Wash was a cheerful, good-natured lad, and, being the smallest of the Sleepers, he usually let the others make the decisions. But before they left Camelot, Elendar had pulled him to one side.

"Wash, my son," he said, "you must be more than a keeper of Sir Reb's armor. He is an impetuous young man, apt to be too trusting. Keep yourself alert. If you see anything that looks suspicious, be sure it's all right before you go on."

Now, thinking of those words, Wash asked sharply, "Don't mean to be unfriendly, but how do we know that you're from Goel?"

"Wash," Reb snapped irritably, "don't be so fussy. Why wouldn't she come from Goel?"

Wash stared at him. "I can think of several reasons. We've got lots of enemies, Reb, and we have to be careful."

"Oh, don't be such a wet blanket! You can tell that this lady is all right."

Mogen listened as they argued. Finally she said, "I think you have a wise counselor. This is a dangerous mission, and you do need to be careful of strangers." She dropped her head for a moment, and when she looked up her eyes were fixed on Reb's.

105

Wash had never seen such dark eyes.

Her voice was soft and soothing. "I only want to be of help, and Goel sends me to be what aid I can."

Ignoring Wash's suspicious looks, Reb said, "Do you have a message from him for us?"

"I have more than that," Mogen said, and a mysterious smile came to her lips. "Goel is apprehensive of the quest and of the challenge you have to face, Sir Reb. He sent me to bring you something that would help." She reached behind her neck and fumbled with something.

It was, Wash saw, a clasp, and she pulled a golden chain over her head and held it out to Reb. "This is what Goel sent me to bring to you."

Reb took the necklace. On the fine chain was mounted a round medallion, also of heavy gold. He blinked at it and held it up to the firelight. "What is this on here?"

"That is the secret sign of Goel. Very few are privileged to know it, and even fewer are privileged to wear this amulet. It came from around the neck of Goel himself."

Wash came forward and looked at the markings on the medallion. The design looked vaguely familiar, but he could not recognize it. He shot a glance at Mogen. "You say Goel himself wears this? I never saw it when I was with him."

"It is unlikely that you would, Wash," Mogen said calmly. "He keeps it beneath his clothes, and only a few know that it exists."

Reb handled the amulet, letting its round form rest in his hand. And as it lay on his palm, something seemed to happen. "Why, this feels warm!" he exclaimed. "Almost as if it's been in the fire."

Mogen nodded. "That is the power of Goel. And that is what I have come to tell you." Her face grew earnest. "You must wear this amulet wherever you go, Sir Reb. It will give you the strength and power you need to over-come the challenge of Sir Baloc." Suddenly she rose to her feet.

Reb and Wash got up quickly too, wondering at her action.

"I must leave you, but promise me you will wear the amulet."

"Leave?" Reb looked around the trackless forest, then back at Mogen. "But where will you go, lady? There's no place around here."

A smile touched her lips again. "I will find my way, but promise me that you will wear the amulet."

Reb fingered again the warm medallion that lay in his hands. He hefted it, then nodded. "Well, if Goel sent it and wants me to wear it, that's all I need to know."

He put it around his neck and slipped it under his clothing. And as he did so, he told Wash later, a strange thing happened. At once he began to feel more powerful. The trees seemed less threatening. He looked at her with astonishment. "Why, this makes me feel like . . . like . . ."

"I know." Mogen smiled. "That is the power of Goel." She grew serious then. "Dangerous things lie ahead of you, Sir Reb. *Never* remove that medallion! Remember, it has the power of Goel in it." Then she gave them one final look. "Farewell for now—but I will not be far from you."

Without another word she walked away, fading into the darkness.

Reb stared after her, then looked at Wash. "Well, I've been to two county fairs and three snake stompin's," he said in amazement, "but I never saw nothing like that!"

Wash's eyes were half shut. He was thinking hard. "Neither did I," he admitted, "and I'm not sure I like it."

"Oh, you'd be suspicious of anybody," Reb said irrita-bly. "Come on now. Why would she come? We've been asking for help from Goel, and now we got it."

Wash sat down and began to poke at the glowing fire.

Reb must have seen the stubbornness on the younger boy's face. He plopped himself down. "I declare, Wash, you'd complain if they hung you with a new rope!"

Wash was more aware than ever of the moaning of the trees and of the oppressive quality of the forest that lay around them. It seemed to close in upon them, worse now than it had ever been. "I don't like it," he said finally. "I don't like this place, and I'm not at all sure that Mogen girl came from Goel."

Reb gave him a disgusted look. "I'm telling you she did, and I don't want to hear any more talk about it."

Wash stared at him, astonished, and Reb tried to explain. "If you had this medallion on *your* neck, you'd know what I'm talking about. Why, it's made a whole new person out of me! I feel like I could tackle *anything!*" He was smiling, and his light blue eyes gleamed in the firelight. He seemed to have become older and taller and stronger— though Wash knew this was an illusion.

Wash saw that it was useless to argue. *He won't listen to me, and there's something about all this I don't understand. I wish Elendar were here!* He finally tossed the stick he was fidgeting with into the fire, got his blankets, and rolled into them. *I don't like any of this, and I wish that girl had never come!*

A vague uneasiness rested on Wash, and he went to sleep only to have bad dreams all night long.

* * *

The next day the two boys continued their journey. Somehow, however, they missed their way. All morning and all afternoon they wandered through the trackless forest.

Finally Wash exclaimed in despair, "I don't think we'll ever get out of here. I've never been so lost in all my life!"

Reb gave him a rough look. "Will you shut up!" he snapped. "All you've done is complain since we left Camelot. Now, either keep your mouth shut, or I'll shut it for you!"

The two had been firm friends, and Wash stared at the face of Reb in amazement. This was not the Reb he knew!

There was a new hardness in the older boy's eyes as he stated, "I'll get us out. Don't worry."

Reb seemed to feel as if he could do anything, Wash thought. He had never been this way before. And Wash wondered if it was indeed the power of the medallion that rested against his chest.

"Come on," Reb said. "We'll go as far as we can before dark."

By dark, sure enough, they had found the track again, and the trail was plainly marked.

* * *

"Baloc's place is right over there. We'll be there tomorrow," Reb said, when they were sitting once more around a campfire. The darkness was again closing in, but here the land was more open, and there was no sound of moaning in the trees. "We'd better go to bed and get a good night's sleep," he advised.

Wash went to sleep at once, but it was difficult for Reb. This strange, excited feeling that was in him kept him awake.

Finally, though, he began to doze and was almost off into a deeper sleep when a voice said, "Reb! Sir Reb, awaken!"

Reb sat up and blinked. The fire was almost dead, but a few stars gave off a cold, frozen light, and then the moon came out from behind a cloud. Sitting across from where he lay was Mogen, her hood thrown back and her eyes glittering in the moonlight.

"Mogen!" he exclaimed. "You're back!"

"Yes, Goel has sent me back to you again. Are you wearing the medallion?"

Reb reached into his shirt and pulled it out. It glittered coldly, despite the heat that it produced. "It sure does make a fellow feel big. I reckon I could take on a dragon, if there were such things."

Mogen smiled, her teeth shining white. "There are things worse than dragons. But as long as you wear the medallion of Goel you do not need to know any fear." She watched as he replaced it, then said, "I have come to give you counsel, for you cannot keep on getting lost in the forest."

"What do you want me to do, Mogen?" he said. "Tell me how to get Elaine back."

"That is why I'm here." She came and sat down beside him. He could smell a faint odor that was strange and exotic and made him a little dizzy. And when he looked into her dark eyes they seemed bottomless pools. "Yes," he whispered, excited by her presence. "You just tell me, and I'll do it."

Suddenly Mogen reached out and put her hands on Reb's temples. Something like an electric current struck him, and he gasped. "What—"

But Mogen began speaking in a language that he did not understand, and he could not seem to move. Her voice was soft and at the same time so powerful that he began to tremble. Though he did not understand the words, he knew that they were important. As he listened, the moon went behind the clouds, casting a darkness over the earth, and only the cold fire of the stars allowed him to look into her eyes.

He never knew how long that exchange went on, and he never knew when she left. But when he awoke she was gone, and he was lying back in his blankets. Still he could feel the pressure of her hands on his head, and the medallion seemed heavier than ever and burned on his chest.

Reb sat up slowly and shook his head. He was frightened and yet excited. "Boy," he breathed. "I never saw anything like her before. But I reckon as long as she's around I can do just about anything I've got to do."

However, when Wash woke up, the first thing he did was blink his eyes and look wildly over at Reb. "What's that smell?" he demanded.

"Smell?" Reb looked puzzled. "I don't smell anything."

Wash's nose wrinkled. "I don't know what it is—it's kind of sharp, but it smells like death to me. The scent of death."

Reb stared. "You just don't know about things, Wash. Come on, this is the day we rescue Elaine!"

12

The Magic Medallion

Wash and Reb stared at each other across the ashes of the campfire. They had risen early, had cooked and eaten breakfast, and during the meal Reb told Wash all that had happened the night before.

He ended by saying, "I tell you, Wash, there never was nothing like her! She's got something in her that I ain't never seen in nobody else in all my born days!" He drew a deep sigh of satisfaction and nodded with assurance. "I don't mind admitting now, I was a little bit afraid of this fellow I've got to beat to get to Princess Elaine— but it's gonna be all right now."

Wash was holding a piece of bread in his hands. He took a small bite and chewed thoughtfully. He had listened carefully to Reb, but there was doubt in his dark brown eyes. He swallowed the morsel and cleared his throat. "I don't know, Reb, it just don't seem right to me somehow."

Reb stared at the small, black lad. "What do you mean?" he asked in surprise. "Here we're out on this quest, and I'm supposed to fight probably the worst and baddest cat in the whole kingdom of Camelot." He grew a little angry. "I'm tellin' you, I need all the help I can get!"

"I know." Wash nodded in agreement. "But not all help is the same, you know."

Reb looked at his friend from under raised eyebrows. "I don't see that," he said firmly. "Any help you get is good—especially in a situation like this."

"But who was she, and where is she now?" Wash glanced around the dense woods. "I didn't hear a thing, and you claim you were talking to her for a long time. Why didn't I wake up?"

"I don't know. I guess you were just too tired. Anyway, it happened just like I told you. Why are you so doubtful about all this, Wash?"

The smaller boy slowly began to gather up the dishes. As he cleaned them, he said, "I don't know—I just got a bad feeling. In the first place, Reb, you still don't know that she came from Goel."

"Of course she did! She told me right off that Goel sent her. And she gave me this." Reaching down, Reb pulled the golden medallion from beneath his shirt and held it up to the light. It caught the golden rays of the early morning sun and glistened in the air. As it turned slowly, Reb said, "As long as I've got this, I'm all right. I can't lose!"

"What's that funny-looking thing on the front of that piece of metal?" Wash asked. He studied it carefully, then said, "That's not the sign of Goel, and it doesn't look like anything I saw in Camelot."

"I don't know," Reb said, "but I know one thing, the second I put it on I felt like a different guy." His eyes glowed, and he smiled triumphantly. "I feel like I'm twenty feet tall and anybody gets in my way better look out, even that Sir Baloc!" He shook himself, got to his feet, and said impatiently, "Come on, Wash. Let's get on our way."

Wash did not argue.

They pulled their gear together, tied it on the packhorse, and climbed into the saddles.

All morning they headed in an easterly direction.

* * *

114

At noon Wash said, "I'm tired, Reb. Let's stop and have something to eat and rest a bit."

"I'm not a bit tired. I could go on all day."

"The horses are tired," Wash snapped. "If you won't think about yourself, think about them."

"Oh, all right." Reb jumped off his horse and watched with some contempt as Wash struggled painfully, almost falling off his animal. "Aren't you ever going to learn to ride a horse?" he complained. "Hurry up and get that food together."

Wash looked at him in surprise, but he said nothing about the boy's sharpness. He put together a scanty meal, and when the two had eaten he said, "Let's just lie down and sleep and let the horses graze a while."

"All right, you lie down. I'll keep watch," Reb said grumpily. He watched Wash throw himself on the ground, then muttered, "I might as well have left you home for all the good you're going to do!"

With a disgruntled look he walked away and sat down, putting his back to a tree. The birds were singing a rather sad, mournful song far off in the forest, and overhead he saw a hawk circling, crossing the blue skies in a searching pattern. The smell of pine and fir was rich in his nostrils, and he took a deep breath. "This is the kind of life for me. I wish I had done this a long time ago."

"I wish you had too, Sir Reb."

"What!" Reb leaped to his feet, his hand on his sword. Then he relaxed as he saw a smiling Mogen emerging from the trees. "You hadn't ought to sneak up on a fellow that way, Mogen," he said reproachfully. "Back in Arkansas a fellow could get hurt doing a trick like that."

"I'm sorry," Mogen said contritely, "but I did want to see you one more time."

"Wait a minute." Reb suddenly turned and looked across at Wash, who had not moved. "Hey, Wash, wake up. You didn't believe what I told you. Now you can see for yourself."

When Wash did not stir, Reb walked over and rolled him onto his back. "Wake up, I said." Then he looked at Mogen with a surprised expression. "Something's wrong with him. He won't wake up."

"He'll be all right as soon as I leave," Mogen said, a strange smile on her lips. She looked very beautiful. She moved to stand beside Reb. "I just helped him to sleep a little bit because I wanted to talk to you alone, Reb."

She put her hand on his arm, and a thrill ran through the boy. He hadn't been around many girls, and this young woman was far more beautiful than any girl he had ever seen. Mogen's voice was soft, and she almost whispered as she said, "I'm proud of you, Sir Reb, and so will everyone else be."

Reb cleared his throat. He could smell the exotic perfume that Mogen wore. He breathed deeply, and it seemed to make him sleepy. Yet, at the same time, it strangely excited him. "Well," he mumbled, "I don't know about that."

Mogen reached up and put her hands on his shoulders. He was tall enough that she had to look up at him. Her lips were rich and red. "All of Camelot will be proud of you when you rescue the Princess Elaine. And here is a reward in advance."

She pulled his head down and kissed him lightly on the lips, then she stepped back, her eyes gleaming. "Now, that will give you something to think about."

Reb's throat was thick, and he had to clear it before he said, "Well, why'd you do that?" And then he muttered, "Never mind. But what I want to know is, how do I find the princess and how do I beat this guy Sir Melchior?"

"That is why I've come to you this morning," Mogen said. "Now listen carefully." She instructed him how to find his way through the woods, and when she had finished, she said, "You'll be challenged, Sir Reb, and, when you are, do not trust in your own strength."

Reb blinked in surprise. "What else would I trust in?"

"Trust in this." Mogen leaned forward and laid her hand over the medallion. She whispered, "This will save you. Hold it up and repeat the words that I will now give you."

Sir Reb was confused. The strange perfume seemed to befuddle him, and the touch of her hand on his chest burned like fire. He listened as she repeated a formula—just a few words. Then, when she stepped back, he swallowed and said, "That's all?"

Mogen smiled mysteriously. "That will be enough," she whispered. "You will see." Then she turned and left abruptly.

Reb was staring after her when Wash's voice came to him. "Well, I didn't mean to sleep so long."

Reb turned to see Wash getting up, rubbing his eyes.

"I guess we'd better be on our way," Wash said.

"You didn't see—"

"I didn't see what?" Wash asked as he started clambering into his saddle. "I was asleep, Reb. So were you, weren't you?"

Reb didn't answer, for he saw at once that Mogen's spell had kept his young friend from seeing her. He wondered about this, but the medallion burned against his chest, and he said roughly, "Come along. It's time to get down to business."

* * *

The challenge came almost without warning. Three knights, dressed in black armor, crested the hill in front of them.

Reb whispered, "Hey, Wash. This looks like trouble!"

"Who are you, and what are you doing in this place?" The tallest of the knights had his visor back, and his cold, gray eyes seemed alive with fire. "Give us your name, boy, and then we will take you captive."

Reb swallowed hard. He knew that any one of them would be more than a match for him, but he could not back down. There was something in him that would not be still. And as the medallion burned his chest he shouted, "You'll not stop me. I've come to get the Princess Elaine. Now give her up, and I'll let you go."

The three knights laughed loudly, and one of them said to their leader, "Let's feed him to the vultures."

"Right. He'll be fit food for them," the tall leader said. "Come!"

The three knights at once leveled their lances and spoke to their horses. They came thundering across the plain.

"Come on, Reb, let's get out of here!" Wash shouted.

Reb had little time to think, but the words of Mogen came back to him, and with a swift gesture he pulled the medallion from beneath his shirt and held it high. He shouted the words that Mogen had given him, then stared amazed.

The knights tumbled out of their saddles as if they had been struck with a club. They hit the ground with a crashing, clanging noise, rolled over and over, and lay still. The dust rose from the ground. Their horses bolted, uttering frightened, neighing sounds.

Wash, who had already half turned his horse, said, "What in the world—"

Fear came upon Reb then, and he galloped forward, thinking that the three might be dead. But he discovered that they were still breathing, and he sighed in relief. At the same time, a fierce pride touched him, pride such as he had never known before. Holding the medallion high, he cried out the strange phrase again.

The three knights climbed to their feet and backed away with terror in their eyes. Then they whirled and ran, crying for mercy.

Wash advanced slowly, his eyes fixed on Reb. He was trembling—he had been afraid of the large armed knights. Now he whispered, "Reb, what happened?"

Reb held up the medal, his eyes glinting with triumph. "Just what I said would happen. I had power I never knew I had before, and now I can take on any knight the Dark Lord sends against me."

Reb's eyes were glowing with some sort of strange light that had never been there before, and his mouth was twisted in a smile that was not a smile.

"I don't like it, Reb," Wash said abruptly. "Whatever it is, it's not right. Let's get out of here."

Reb glared at him. "You may as well go back to Camelot, Wash," he said contemptuously. "But I'm going to get the Princess Elaine."

He turned his horse and spurred away.

Wash stared after him. "Ain't nothing good gonna come out of this—I know that much! But I've come this far, and I reckon Goel would have me go the rest of the way. So come on, horse, let's go!"

* * *

Elaine sat in the small room where she was held by Sir Baloc. When he first took her, she had been filled with blind panic, and even now, when the huge knight came around, she felt fear rise in her throat. But she refused to let him see that fear.

She looked up now as he entered, his dark eyes fixed on her. "Well, Princess," he said, "are you ready to agree to marry me?"

"Never," Elaine said firmly, lifting her chin. "I demand that you take me home immediately."

Baloc threw his head back and laughed. "That will never happen. But I'll tell you what *will* happen. That shallow young stripling you were so fond of, or so I hear—what's his name? Reb?—he's on his way to rescue you."

She started at that, and he grinned. He drew his sword, held it up, and tested the edge. "When I get through with him, his shoulders will be lonesome for his head!"

"My father will send the whole army of his knights to get me!"

"No, he's afraid, because he knows how strong we've gotten. So he sent one challenger." Again Baloc laughed. "And I can't think of a better one. If they'd sent some of the older knights, we may have had trouble—but not with this weak-kneed foreigner. Come on!" Sir Baloc grabbed Elaine's wrist and dragged her, effortlessly, out of the room.

"Where are we going? Where are you taking me?" She fought against him, but he merely looked at her as he would at a feeble kitten. "I'm putting you outside for bait. I want Sir Reb to get a good look at you. My men tell me he's just over the hill."

Elaine felt great hope, and yet at the same time doubt came, for she knew the power of the man who held her. *Reb will never stand a chance against him. Very few of my father's knights could stand up to Baloc.*

He yanked her along and stopped under a tree. "There he is," he said suddenly. "Now watch this, my lady."

Elaine watched Sir Baloc walk over to where his groom had his battle horse ready. He was lifted into the saddle, and he put the crested helmet over his head. Then he took the lance.

"This won't take long." He gave a loud cry and said, "Now, Sir Reb, you'll see what it means to meet the pow-

120

ers of the Dark Lord's servants!" He touched his spurs to the horse and galloped straight at Reb.

Elaine did not see clearly what happened, but she saw Reb hold up something that caught the glint of the sunlight and heard him cry out some strange words. At the same time Sir Baloc pulled his horse up sharply. Then he uttered a hoarse cry, turned, and galloped away as if all the knights of the kingdom were after him.

Elaine gasped and shock ran over her.

Then, suddenly, Reb was there! He leaned from his horse and said, "Princess Elaine, are you all right?"

"Oh, yes," she said quickly. Then she looked after the fleeing Baloc in bewilderment. "But what happened? Why did he run away?"

"He was afraid that he would die, so he ran—like the coward that he is." He laughed aloud, and there was a note of victory in his voice as he said, "Come along, Princess. I'll get you a horse, and we'll get you back to your family."

* * *

When Sir Reb led the Princess Elaine through the gates of Camelot, a cry went up such as had not been heard in many a year. The air was filled with hats thrown up by jubilant men, and a pressing throng surrounded the pair as they made their way toward the castle.

Reb had removed his armor, and Wash was following far behind with the pack animal.

Wash was joined almost at once by Elendar, who appeared out of nowhere. "How did this happen, my son?" Elendar demanded.

Wash shook his head. "I don't know. I never saw nothing like it." He related how the three knights had fallen from their saddles and Sir Baloc had run in fear. "And it's all that medallion he wears around his neck and the

121

funny words he says. And he keeps talking about this woman named Mogen who's taught him how to do all this."

"*Mogen,* you say?" Elendar's eyes glinted fiercely. "I don't like the sound of that."

"I did the best I could," Wash said miserably, "but he wouldn't listen to me. I wish you'd been there, Elendar."

Elendar's hand fell on the boy's shoulder, and he clasped it firmly. "Never mind. You have a good spirit, my boy. Now we must be very careful to see that your friend doesn't take harm from this."

Wash looked at the crowds who were screaming Reb's name and saw the pair dismount in front of the king and queen. Elaine rushed forward and was embraced by her parents, who, in turn, fell upon Sir Reb and seemed to be crying.

Wash wagged his head. "It looks to me like Reb is in pretty solid. He rescued the princess, and that's what's important, isn't it?"

"Winning is not always important," Elendar said slowly. He looked tired and suddenly bowed his shoulders. "It's how we win that counts—and I very much fear that we have not seen the last of all this."

"Who is Mogen, and what's this thing that gives Reb all that power?" Wash asked. "Is it from Goel, do you think?"

"No, never from Goel. He doesn't use magic. He uses men and women—and young people," he added as he put his hands on Wash's shoulders again.

"Then what's wrong?"

Elendar did not answer for a long moment, and when he did his voice was so low that Wash barely heard it. "Sometimes the dark forces of this world use people as well."

13

The Curse of the Dragon

Y ou know, Jake, Reb always was stubborn. But ever
since he brought Princess Elaine back, he's been different."

Jake Garfield was standing beside Josh, his hands in
his pockets. He looked small beside the tall boy, and his
red hair and brown eyes formed a vivid contrast.

Jake agreed. "That's right. He's just not the same
guy we've always known and liked."

"Oh, you two are just jealous." Abbey sniffed. She
looked over to where Reb and Princess Elaine were talking underneath a brilliant banner. They stood on the jousting field, and Reb had just toppled another of the king's
ablest knights. Abbey sighed and rolled her eyes. "He's so
strong. But I don't see how he stands up to those big men
the way he does."

Sarah gave her a critical glance. "I think there's a little more to it than we know," she said. "Wash, I've never
believed that you told us everything about how you two
managed to get Princess Elaine back. And Reb won't say
anything either. What actually went on?"

Wash wanted to tell, but Elendar had sworn him to
silence. "I guess I'll have to let Reb do the talking—if he
wants to," he said finally.

Dave Cooper came up just in time to hear this. He
looked over toward Reb, and there was bitterness in his
eyes. He was fully as tall and even stronger than Bob Lee
Jackson, but he had been cast into the background by the
accomplishments of the young Southerner. "Well, I think

he's going to have to be taught a lesson. He's gotten so proud he's not the same guy we once knew."

A murmur went around the group, but Josh said, "Wait a minute. We can't lose control of this thing. I know Reb has been a little hard to get along with, but most of us would be if we'd gotten the kind of attention that he's gotten. After all, he came out of nowhere to become the king's favorite."

"That's what I say," Abbey agreed. She looked at Reb again and sighed. Always the romantic, she added, "Wouldn't it be something if Reb married the Princess Elaine and became king of Camelot?"

"Nobody's going to become king of *anything* unless the Dark Lord is stopped. I don't know what happened, but I'm going to find out," Josh snapped. He looked over at the couple, then shrugged. "No sense trying to talk to him. If he won't listen to Elendar, he won't listen to anyone." He scratched his head and said, "It's like he's been —*bewitched!* But we'll have to do the best we can. Goel sent us here to do something, and at least Reb's gotten the princess back. I'll give him that much."

* * *

At that moment Princess Elaine was saying, "Reb, I wish I could tell you how grateful I am for what you've done. I'd just about given up hope. That awful Baloc!" She shivered. "It makes me almost sick to think about him."

Reb smiled and patted her shoulder with a freedom he never would have used at an earlier date. "You don't have to worry about him anymore," he said loftily. "If he does show up, I'll put the run on him."

"Put the run on him?" Elaine stared. "What does that mean?"

"Oh, just a saying we had back in Arkansas. Means I'll run him out of here."

Elaine chewed her lower lip. "I still don't understand what happened. Can't you tell me about it, Reb?"

Reb hesitated, then shook his head. "I suppose some things are better not talked about," he said grandly.

The truth was that he had had more visits from Mogen, and she had cautioned him not to speak of what they did together. Each time she had come, he felt the power flow out of her hands, and when she spoke strange words over him he felt tall enough to smite the sun.

Now he looked down at Elaine. "I don't want you worrying, Princess. Whatever that Dark Lord throws at us, I'll throw right back in his face."

Elaine watched Reb carefully as he moved away. Something about him was different. Something that she didn't understand. "He's not the same as he used to be," she whispered to herself. "Somehow he's stronger—and yet he's weaker too. I just don't understand it. Maybe Elendar can explain."

She went to find Elendar, and as she did so she was aware that she was somehow disappointed in Reb and afraid for him even after all he had done.

* * *

As Reb was proclaiming what he would do to the servants of the Dark Lord, Sir Melchior was receiving a visit from one he was not happy to see.

He had been dozing in his chair, almost asleep, in the privacy of his quarters, when without warning a figure materialized in front of him.

"What!" Melchior leaped to his feet and grabbed at a sword that hung on the wall. Flipping it out of its sheath, he turned to face the figure, who was clothed from head to foot in a long gray cloak.

"Who are you?" he challenged. "And how did you get past my guards?"

A deep, mellow voice answered, "You need not blame the guards, Melchior. They could not have stopped me in any case."

Melchior blinked at the assurance of the voice, took one step forward, and lifted his sword. "Who are you? Quick, or I'll have your head from your body!"

"My name is not important. What is important is the one I serve—the same one that you serve."

Melchior swallowed and lowered the point of his blade. "The Dark Lord?" he whispered, and a chill suddenly went over him, for he could feel the piercing glance of the eyes that were almost hidden by the cowling. "What is your message?"

"You will come with me, and I will show you."

Melchior had little desire to go with such a deadly visitor. But he knew enough of the Dark Lord to understand that protests would be futile. "Very well," he said, trying to put assurance into his voice, "I'll call my guards."

"They would not hear you." The visitor came forward and put his hands suddenly on Melchior's shoulders. They were icy cold and gripped with a power that Melchior had not dreamed existed. He tried to cry out, but the room suddenly swirled around him, and he felt himself passing into a fit of unconsciousness.

* * *

"Awake, Melchior!"

When Melchior opened his eyes, he looked around wildly. "Where *is* this place?" he demanded of his captor. "Why have you brought me here?"

"To show you how we shall overcome the Sword and Kingdom of Camelot."

Melchior looked around. He was in a cave, but such a huge cavern he had never before seen. There was semi-darkness all about him, and yet, far down a long tunnel, he saw light. "What is that?"

"That is what I have brought you to see." The Dark Lord's servant motioned and turned. He walked toward the light, and Melchior, frightened to be alone, preferring even the company of this servant, hurried to keep up.

He found himself brought up short when the dark-clad figure put out a hand and held him back. "Not too close," he said. Then he pointed. "There. There is the bane of King Dion and of Camelot!"

Melchior leaned forward to look over a precipice. They had arrived at a huge pit, illuminated by torches stuck around the wall at intervals. It must have been two hundred feet wide and at least one hundred feet deep, and there, at the bottom, was . . .

"What *is* that thing?" Melchior gasped.

"That is what some would call a dragon. It is not, actually, but is a beast that the Dark Lord has bred for just such times as these—and for his own amusement."

Melchior stared in cold fear at the huge beast. It had a long neck and powerful claws. He shuddered at the huge bat wings and snakelike head. The beast raised his head and uttered a hoarse cry.

"Quick, back!" The servant of the Dark Lord jerked Melchior away from the chasm. "One drop of his venom and—untreated—you will die. It is poisonous!"

Melchior began to tremble. He wiped his forehead with a shaking hand. "What does this all mean?"

A hollow laugh came from the darkness of the hood, and Melchior could see the cruel lips turn up in an evil smile. "This is your weapon, Melchior. See that you use it well. Loose this beast on the country, and you will see that nothing can stand before him."

"Me? Why I wouldn't get within a hundred feet of that thing!"

"You will be safe with this." The cloaked servant handed him a black baton.

It seemed to be a simple wand, and yet, when Melchior took it in his hand, he felt it quiver with energy. "What is it?" he gasped.

"You would not understand if I told you, but it will control the dragon. Command and point the wand, and he will attack whatever is in front of him."

Melchior gulped, but he knew he had little choice. "What if he turns on me?"

"He will not. He is under the command of the Dark Lord. That wand in your hand is the symbol of the power that will control him. Quickly now, loose the power of the dragon, and we will see what King Dion and his precious knights of chivalry will do against the Dark Lord."

* * *

The village of Denmore awakened at its usual hour. The men were moving sleepily about the streets. The children were playing, rolling, fighting, crying aloud. The women emerged to do their chores, and some of the peasants had gone to the well and were washing their clothes.

It was a typical, warm spring morning filled with the cries of the children, the sounds of women laughing at the well, and the voices of men calling to each another as they worked in the fields.

Suddenly a keen whistling sound split the air.

Startled, the villagers looked up to see a dark shape appear by a growth of small trees. A cry of fear went up from the children, who scattered and ran to their mothers or into the woods.

"What is it?" the chief villager, a man named Minton, cried. Then his eyes grew wide, and he gasped. "It's a wild beast! Get your arrows, bows, your swords!"

The men rushed for their weapons. Minton himself grabbed his bow and fitted an arrow to the string. As the hideous beast fell screaming down upon him, he loosed it. The arrow struck the scaly armor of the dragon and was deflected. Then the creature breathed a venomous fog from its huge mouth. The vapor blew out like live steam and surrounded Minton, who dropped his bow, grabbed his throat, fell to the ground, and grew still.

Upon seeing this, the other men threw down their weapons and ran. Some were killed as they fled. Women died too, and even children, as the dragon ravaged the village.

When the beast flew away, seeming to heed some faraway call, the village clerk came out from beneath a log, his face covered with dirt. Fear made his eyes wide, and he gasped, "Quick, my horse! I must go to the king! He must know that evil is loose in Camelot!"

14
The Pride of Sir Reb

Sometimes fear can sweep over an entire nation exactly as it does over a single individual. So it was in the land of Camelot. As the fierce and deadly beast struck village after village, panic fell over all the inhabitants. Even the flight of a crow overhead was sufficient for men, women, and children to drop their tools and run screaming for shelter.

There was no pattern to the attacks. The creature might strike in the eastern sector one day, fall out of sight, then move on the western sector a week later.

"I tell you," King Dion shouted to his council, "the thing must be killed!" His face was pale with anger, and he tugged fiercely at his mustache as he paced back and forth before the elders.

They stared at him anxiously.

"Sire," Sir Gwin said, "we have sent our best knights to do battle with this *thing*—three of them." His face grew long. "None of them survived. Witnesses tell us that though they faced up bravely to the creature, all their strength and courage went for naught. The beast either sank his teeth into them or overwhelmed them with his breath."

King Dion ordinarily was the kindest of men. Rarely did he speak harshly to his subjects, but he was beside himself, and now he shouted with rage. "Are you a coward, Gwin? Are you afraid to face this beast yourself?"

Sir Gwin's face went pale. He straightened up. "I tell you, no man ever accused me of cowardice, Your Majesty."

"That's right, my dear," Queen Mauve said quickly and laid a restraining hand on her husband's arm. "It seems that this monster cannot be defeated with ordinary weapons."

The king stared at her, and some of the anger left him. "Of course, my dear, you are right." He shot a quick look at Sir Gwin and gave his apology. "I spoke too harshly, Sir Gwin. I know only too well that your courage is exceeded by none in my kingdom."

A murmur went around the council, and for a while the talk grew more and more dark and pessimistic.

Finally, the eldest member of the council said, "It would be well, Your Majesty, would it not, to ask our visitors the Seven Sleepers to enter into council with us? After all, they are sent to us from Goel."

Prince Loren shook his head. "I don't see that they can help," he said stubbornly. "If our best knights have failed, what can mere children do?"

Princess Elaine was sitting beside him. She had said nothing during the council. She never did. It was not her place, she felt. But now, suddenly, she spoke up. "I think we must look to Elendar to lead us in this crisis. He is the one who knows the Dark Lord and his ways best, and I think he knows the Sleepers well."

Every eye turned to the tall form of Elendar, who was standing back in the shadows. He wore a simple cloak of white linen, and his white hair well matched it. Only his eyes seemed dark and glowing. He looked at Princess Elaine, and a smile smoothed away the sternness of his lips. "My Princess," he said, "I thank you for your confidence—but I am not certain of what course to take."

The king stared bleakly at him. "If *you* are not certain, Elendar, what are the rest of us to do?"

Elendar lowered his head and seemed to examine the floor. All were aware that he was thinking profoundly, and they had grown so accustomed to waiting on his wisdom that the silence grew thick even as it grew longer.

Finally Elendar said, "The Princess Elaine may be more right than all of us. I do not claim to know the ways of Goel better than any other. But one thing I do know—when he sends a messenger, there is power in that messenger." He stopped and nodded firmly. "He has sent us seven messengers. I think it well to pay heed to what they might say." He looked hard at Prince Loren. "*Children* they are not. They are wise and have been tried in the hard school of adversity. They have remained faithful to Goel when others have faltered. I say, call the Seven Sleepers!"

* * *

Sir Gwin approached Josh Adams. "Josh, you and the others are summoned to the High Council."

Josh stared at him, disconcerted. "It's about the dragon, isn't it?" he asked.

"Isn't everything about that frightful beast these days?" Sir Gwin replied grimly. "Yes. Come quickly. The council is waiting."

Josh whirled, called the rest, and when they were together he said, "The king and the council have sent for us." He added carefully, "It's about this dragon."

"I never believed in such a thing as dragons," Dave said. "But we've seen strange things in Nuworld. Nothing much stranger than this, though."

"What can he want with us?" Jake asked. He ruffled his red hair and pulled at it nervously. "From what I hear, this thing eats knights for breakfast." He thought for a moment and said, "I wish I had an AK-7 attack rifle. I'd stop his clock."

"Well, you don't have," Reb had come in late and listened as Josh explained the problem. Now, instead of waiting—as he would have done earlier—he said, "Come along, we can't keep the king waiting."

Sarah fell in beside Josh and saw the set look on his face. "Don't be upset, Josh," she whispered. "Reb doesn't mean to be so bossy."

"Yes, he does," Josh said grimly. "He means exactly that. He's gotten unbearable, and I don't know what to do about it." He looked miserable. "If he can whip full-grown knights, what chance would I have to make him listen to me? He'd pound me into the ground."

Sarah said quickly, "Now, Josh, don't say that. One thing we've both learned from being in this place and serving Goel is that power is not always the answer. Time and time again we've seen Goel send the mighty into the dust, haven't we now? So you just stop putting yourself down. You hear me?"

Josh glanced over and took in Sarah's flashing eyes. He grinned. "You always were bossy. What would you do if you didn't have me to boss around?"

Sarah sniffed. "I am not bossy. I just think you need to realize who you are, that's all. Come on now, let's see what the king has to say."

* * *

The Seven Sleepers filed in front of the long table where the council sat.

The king looked up. "Stand not upon ceremony. We have no time to waste. You're wondering why we've called you all together."

Reb said at once, "Why, Your Majesty, it has to be about this dragon. That's all anyone's talking about."

Dion gazed at the tall young man and nodded. "That's right, Sir Reb. The kingdom is going to fall apart if something isn't done. Elendar's suggested that we bring you Sleepers here. Elendar, you speak to them."

Elendar stepped forward. "No man knows the mind of Goel except as he chooses to reveal himself. But we know that he does not do things foolishly, and we know that he never fails. Therefore, I have to assume that you seven have been sent to Camelot to perform a task. The only question is, how is this task to be accomplished?"

Silence fell across the room.

Finally the quiet was broken by Reb, who said rather loudly, "Why, I reckon I know the answer to that."

He watched the eyes of Elendar unblinkingly. He had met with Mogen the night before. She stayed with him long and told him that this was going to happen—that he would be called upon, that the king would ask the Sleepers to do something about the threat to the kingdom, and she had whispered, "This is your chance—not only to win more favor with the king but to win more than that."

"More than that?" Reb answered. "What could that be?"

Mogen smiled. "Power lies within your grasp, Reb. Don't let it slip from you. Men will do anything for power, and I want you to have it. Why, it's not beyond reason that you might one day rule this whole kingdom."

At one time this would have seemed foolish to Reb, but since meeting Mogen and since she had been coming to him in the dark hours of the night, he had changed greatly. He simply smiled. "Well, I reckon I could handle it, if it comes to that."

He had not seen her evil smile behind her hand, and now as he faced the council he felt large and powerful and strong. The medallion burned on his chest as he said, "I'll fight this dragon. He can't stand before me."

"Reb," Josh broke in, appalled, "that's not for you to say."

"Indeed, I would not like to see you meet this beast," King Dion said. "You've proved your courage, young man, many times, but this beast is more than any man can defeat. The prophecy came forth long ago that no man born of woman could defeat the monster created by the Dark Lord. We all feel that this is the monster that was spoken of, and therefore you would be killed if you attempted to fight it."

"Right now is the time to hit him!" Reb cried out. He clapped his hand on his sword, drew it, and brandished it in the air. "I will kill this varmint for you, Your Majesty! I know it!"

* * *

Elendar half closed his eyes at Reb's words, but King Dion gasped in astonishment. "Why, Sir Reb—I believe you might do it. I don't know why, but somehow, even as you speak, I feel power coming out of you."

The elders all nodded. Their leader stood and said, "Let the young man try his strength against that of the dragon."

King Dion hesitated only one moment. Then he agreed. "Yes, let it be so. Sir Reb," he said, "if you succeed in your quest, you will be the foremost knight in all of Camelot."

Sir Gwin frowned at that and shot a glance at Prince Loren, who sat silent, his face pale.

Josh was standing where he could see the prince's face. *Pretty hard on Prince Loren, to be put aside in favor of a stranger,* he thought. *But he wouldn't have any more chance against that dragon than I would.*

The king came to stand before Sir Reb. He put his hand on the boy's shoulder. "Sir Reb, you may choose any here to accompany you."

But Reb seemed filled with the feeling of power. He shook his head. "I'll get right at it!" He whirled and left the room.

The king stared after him. He turned then to the other Sleepers. "May Goel be with him! For if he is not, he has no chance."

Josh felt great fear, for he had learned to love Bob Lee Jackson. True, of late he had been somewhat swollen with pride, but that did not change what the two had shared. When they were outside the king's chambers, Josh said, "I'm going to go as his squire. Perhaps I can do something."

But when he caught up with Reb, Reb said simply, "No, Josh. You need to stay here with the other Sleepers. I can take care of this myself. I've decided not even to take a squire."

Josh replied quietly, "Reb, something is . . . wrong with you. You're not the same as you used to be."

"I should hope not." Reb laughed. "I was a pretty sorry specimen when I first got here! Now I'm the king's favorite—and likely to be more!"

Josh squinted, searching Reb's face. "That's what I mean. That's exactly the sort of thing Bob Lee Jackson would never have said. It's like—" he hesitated "—it's like somebody else has got inside of you."

For one moment Reb's eyes widened, but then he said, "You're dreaming, Josh." He patted Josh on the shoulder. "You take care of things here. After I've knocked this dragon off, we'll have a long talk about the way things are going to be."

Reb walked away, and Josh turned back to where the rest of the group were waiting.

"Josh," Sarah said, "could you talk any sense into him?"

"He won't listen." He turned to Princess Elaine, who had joined Sarah. "Couldn't *you* talk to him, Princess? He thinks a lot of you."

Elaine looked after the departing young man. A thought seemed to come to her, but instead of speaking she slipped silently away.

"She can't do any more than the rest of us," Dave said.

"Sure wish I had that attack rifle," Jake muttered.

"It'd take a Stealth Bomber to knock *that* thing out!" Wash said.

"Are you going as his squire?" Abbey asked Josh.

"No. I asked him, but he wouldn't let me. He thinks he doesn't need any help." He looked around sadly. "I'm afraid for him. Something's in him that shouldn't be there, and it's gonna get him killed."

15

Encounter with a Dragon

Elaine awakened out of a fitful sleep. She had tossed and turned and had drifted off only once or twice. When the sun barely had begun to turn the blackness of the eastern sky to a misty gray, she arose from her bed. Slipping into a robe, she walked out of her chamber, past the guard, and into the outer court.

For a long time she walked back and forth, for she had been troubled by thoughts of the crisis that had fallen upon Camelot. She thought of the horrible beast that had come to plague the kingdom and was troubled by Reb's insistence on going forth to do battle with him.

The first red light of morning drew a line against the eastern horizon as she stood at a parapet overlooking the castle grounds.

Suddenly she was aware of someone on the balcony with her! Thinking it was a servant, she turned and started to speak, then halted abruptly. A man she had never seen before stood there.

Her heart lurched with fear. "Who are you? What do you want?"

In the murky light of morning the man advanced, and when Elaine retreated he threw back the cowl that hid his face. "Do not fear, my daughter," he said quietly.

Something in the strong, clean features of her visitor took away the apprehension that had filled Elaine. He was very tall and had light brown hair that fell to his shoulders. His age was indeterminate. Though he was not old, he seemed mature beyond his outer appearance. Something in the depths of his gray eyes spoke of wisdom and calmness like the mountains far to the west—solid, steady, immovable.

He waited as she regained her composure, then said, "My name is Goel."

"Goel!" Elaine felt the power of the presence of the one about whom she had heard so much. She could not speak for a moment. Then she curtsied deeply, and from that position, bowing her head, she whispered, "I welcome you, my lord."

Goel approached and put out his hand. When Elaine took it, he lifted her to her feet. "You have been a faithful handmaiden of your father and mother, Princess." His voice ran deep, and there was surety in it and gladness despite its tone. "Now," he added, "I have come to ask that you be *my* handmaiden."

"Me!" Elaine gasped. "But, my lord, I am not worthy to be the servant of Goel!"

"Every woman and girl I call to be my servant," Goel said. Sadness came into his fine eyes as he added in a grieved tone, "Not all I call will answer. But all women are called, as are all men." He studied her face, then smiled. "I see that you are ready, and I am pleased with you, my daughter."

Elaine felt that his eyes were going past her outward form, that he was reading the impulses of her heart, and she experienced a flash of joy as she said in wonder, "Why, I have waited for you all my life, Goel, but I didn't even know what I was waiting for!"

"I am glad you feel that way," he said quietly. "Now, I have come to call you to a difficult task—one that many strong men would hesitate to dare."

"What is it, Sire?"

"You are part of a plan that I have devised to save

140

your father's kingdom. The Dark Powers are afoot, and now the danger is great."

"You mean the dragon."

"The beast is only a part. The Dark Lord's arm is long. He has many deadly servants—and unless something is quickly done, Camelot will fall under his sway."

"I will do anything you command, Lord Goel," Elaine said at once. She saw a smile come to his lips. "But I am not able to do much."

"You are able to believe in me and to obey my word," Goel answered, "and that is more than you know, Princess." His face grew very serious. "Listen carefully. I will tell you what you must do."

* * *

At the moment Goel was visiting Elaine, Bob Lee Jackson, too, had a visitor.

He had risen early and was preparing his equipment to ride out of Camelot. He had determined to take no squire with him but to go alone. He finished saddling Thunder and was about to swing into the saddle when suddenly Mogen was there.

He started. She had the habit of appearing seemingly out of nowhere. But he was glad to see her. He had reached the point where he grew apprehensive when she did *not* appear. Once he had said to himself, *Reb Jackson, you're getting to be pretty bad. If you don't see Mogen regular, you're afraid of your own shadow.*

This troubled him, for he had always been a self-sufficient young man. But now, this woman had grown to be something of an addiction for him. He *had* to see her, and he felt uncertain when he could not.

She came at various times, sometimes in dreams and visions, often speaking strange things into his ear that he could barely remember when he came out of sleep. His dreams when she came to him were troublesome, frightening, and filled with shapes that he could never quite remember but that would have been nightmarish had he seen them in his waking hours.

"Sir Reb," Mogen said.

Her gown surprised him. Oftentimes she wore black, but this morning she was clothed entirely in a white garment that gleamed in the morning sun. Her eyes were shaded by some thought, and he felt again the power of her glance.

"It is time for you to prove yourself and the power that is in you."

Even as she spoke, Reb felt the medallion begin to glow against his chest. He had taken it off the night before to bathe and was shocked at the fear he felt when it was not around his neck. Quickly he put it on again and drew a sigh of relief.

Now he touched it. "What *is* this medallion, Mogen? Why do I feel so powerful when I wear it and so . . . so lost when I take it off? It's as though it has become a part of me."

Mogen's lips curved upward. "Do not fear. It *has* become a part of you, but it has given you power, and that is what you need." She came closer. "The hour has come for you to prove yourself and the power of the medallion. You will see soon the source of this great power. You and I, together, will do marvelous things in Camelot, once you have done this."

Reb said hoarsely, "What will we do?"

"We will rule together, you and I," Mogen whispered. And then she stepped back. "Now, one more task. You will go to meet the dragon, and, when you go, remember the power that lies within the medallion."

She spoke to him for some time, then put her hands on his cheeks and began a chant, using as usual words he did

142

not understand. But as she spoke, they flowed over him, touching the deepest springs in his heart. They frightened him and yet exalted him at the same time. Finally she stopped.

"Let's go now. To the Valley of the Stone. Do you know it?"

"I know where it is. Sir Gwin said it is best not to go there." He added hastily, "He said the place was haunted, but I thought that was just superstition."

She did not answer at once, then said, "There are strange things in that valley, but there you will meet the dragon, and there you must overcome. Remember, when you meet the dragon, hold up the medallion and cry out with all of your heart that which I have given you today. Go quickly now, and when you return, Camelot will be ours."

She stepped back, and Reb watched as she turned and disappeared around the corner of a building. He thought, *I can't figure out where she stays. She's always there, but it's like she suddenly appears from nowhere.*

Quickly he arranged his armor on the packhorse, mounted Thunder, and started to ride out. When he reached the city gate, he was met by someone he had never seen before.

"Who's that?" Reb asked sharply.

"I'm your squire for this journey, Sir Reb." The speaker was mounted on a small gray horse and was clad in Lincoln green. The rider's cloak covered his form, and his face was hidden by the cowling that was drawn over it.

"I need no squire," Reb said. "Who are you?"

"I am sent by Goel," was the answer.

"Goel?" Reb started. The sound of the name sent a sudden shaft of fear through him that he could not explain. He had always loved Goel, had been the most interested of all the Seven in the stories of the leader they followed. "Where is he?"

"He will not be far away. Now his command is that I follow you."

Reb leaned forward, trying to look into the face of the speaker. He hesitated. Something in him said to refuse the offer, but he could not refuse Goel. He wondered why Mogen had said nothing of this. Finally, unable to decide, he said gruffly, "Come along if you're coming. We're going to the Valley of the Stone. Are you afraid?"

"No," was the quiet answer. "I am not afraid."

"Come on, then." Reb spurred his mighty horse forward. Deliberately he tried to outdistance his follower, but every time he looked back, there the smaller horse was with the rider cloaked in green.

* * *

The Valley of the Stone was so called because of a massive stone, a black rock, that pointed toward the sky like a huge finger.

As Reb rode past the stone, he felt a vibration that seemed to shake the earth. If he had been apprehensive before, now he knew that this valley was not a normal place. But he touched the medallion on his chest and felt its familiar power flow through him, and once again he pressed forward.

The valley was filled with many stones and small clumps of trees—scrub oak mostly—and deep gullies that cut across its surface. Carefully he guided Thunder along the lips of the ravines, always alert, scanning the sky, for he knew that from there the dragon would appear. From time to time he glanced back and saw the rider in green silently following.

I wonder who that is? he asked himself. Then he shrugged. *He won't be any help in a fight, that's for sure.*

He had noted that the rider carried a bow and a quiver of arrows but was aware that they would be of little use.

What Reb himself carried was a long lance that Mogen had told him was charmed. "All you have to do is pierce the beast with the tip, and he will die."

The sun was high in the sky when Reb suddenly heard a faint whistling to his right. Looking up, he saw a speck just over the trees. That speck grew larger, and the whistling grew louder, until he recognized it as the keening noise that many witnesses of the dragon had spoken of. He held his lance firmly and urged Thunder forward.

Then he decided to fight on foot. Stepping off his horse, he looked back and called to the squire, "Hold this hoss while I kill this varmint!"

The rider in green came forward and dismounted but said nothing.

Reb said, "Those arrows won't help you none—not against that thing."

"I will do what I can," was the answer.

Reb again tried to see his face but could not.

The monster drew close. Reb ran forward a few steps, and then the air seemed full of the sound of the screaming beast. Suddenly it was in front of him. Fully twenty feet high, the beast reared up, slender of body but with flaming red eyes and a mouth full of gleaming teeth— white and sharp as sabers.

Fear tried to creep over Reb, but he advanced toward the dragon.

The beast reared again, its glinting scales catching the sun. Its white underbelly was revealed, and Reb picked the spot where he would plant his lance.

Got to get close enough to put this spear in that varmint. He held his shield high, and when the screaming creature started toward him, tail whipping madly and ven-

145

omous froth falling from its fangs, he muttered, "Can't let him get those teeth into me, but got to get closer!"

The beast suddenly lunged. Reb threw up his arm and took the driving force of the serpentlike head on his shield. But the impact drove him backward. He dropped both shield and lance and fell sprawling.

The beast reared up over him. There was a scream of victory from its open jaws.

And then Reb remembered. The medallion! The moment had arrived. He thrust a hand under his shirt. Bringing forth the amulet, he held it high and cried out the formula that Mogen had given him.

He fully expected to see the beast fall down dead—but nothing happened! Again he cried the words, but the medallion, he saw, had grown dull.

Then, to one side, the form of Mogen suddenly materialized. She was dressed this time in black, with her hood thrown back.

Reb cried out, "Mogen, help me!"

Mogen did not move, and somehow she seemed to grow older, her face lengthening and her eyes turning into mere slits.

What's happening? Reb thought wildly, and he called out again. "Help me! The medallion isn't working!"

"You fool!" Mogen laughed, but it was a cackle, not the smooth laugh of the girl he had come to know. She seemed transformed into an old woman! Her fingers had grown into long claws, her face was wrinkled, her mouth twisted into a cruel sneer. "Now you know who I am. You were such an easy prey. Now you will taste what it is like to be under the power of the Dark Lord!"

"The Dark Lord! But you said you were from Goel!"

"No," Mogen sneered. "I have nothing to do with Goel." Then she cackled again. "Now taste the teeth of the dragon."

Reb turned quickly and saw the beast move toward him at a sign from the witch—as he now knew Mogen to be. He rolled to his feet and seized his lance. And, as the dragon dropped his evil head forward, Reb struck.

But the point of the lance slid off the breast of the beast. The monster's teeth snapped at him. Reb threw up his arm and felt searing pain as the teeth sank into it. *The poison—I'm a goner!*

He tried to retreat, but the dragon, with a powerful sweep of its head, threw him rolling in the dirt. He saw that his arm was torn. Already he felt the poison beginning to work, going quickly through his whole body like molten fire. *I'm dying, and it's too late!*

At that moment Mogen cried, "Stay away! Who are you?"

Reb opened his eyes to see the squire who had followed him. His eyes were swimming now with pain, but he saw the squire stop and nock a silver arrow into his bow.

"Very well, you fool. You can die with him!"

"I won't die," the youthful voice said calmly.

Mogen shouted, "You do not know the ancient prophecy! No man can stand before this beast!"

And then Reb heard a clear voice cry out, "But I am no man! I am Princess Elaine, daughter of the king of Camelot!"

Shock coursed through Reb's body. He struggled up onto one elbow. Dimly he saw the green cloak thrown back, and there was the face of Elaine. Reb could scarcely breathe. "Go back," he whispered hoarsely. "Go back, Elaine. He'll kill you!"

"No, I shall slay *him*," Elaine cried. She cocked the bow with the silver arrow in it, and as the beast rose up with a mighty scream, preparing to launch himself forward, her voice rose clear. "Die by the power of Goel!" And she released the fully drawn bow.

The arrow streaked through the air and struck the beast on its underside, piercing the armor and disappearing down to the feathers.

Reb felt himself slipping away fast, but he heard the beast utter an awful, screeching cry and saw it fall to one side, thrashing about as it died.

He also heard Mogen screaming in rage and Elaine's clear challenge, "Begone, foul witch! Or you will meet the fate of your creature!"

Then Reb felt cool hands on his face, and even as blackness was overwhelming him he heard a voice saying, "Reb, Reb! Do not die!"

He opened his eyes one moment. Elaine's features swam into focus, and he tried to smile. "I reckon it's too late for me . . ."

16
The Darkest Hour

He—he looks so pale, and he's hardly breathing at all."
Josh stood beside the still form of Reb. The rest of
the Sleepers circled his bed. They had been admitted to
his hospital room only a few minutes before and now were
in shock at their friend's condition.

Josh swallowed hard and looked up at the man in the
blue physician's coat who stood back by the wall. "How is
he, Doctor?" he asked.

The doctor, a tall man with dark eyes and olive com-
plexion, studied the young man on the bed and shook his
head. "Not well—not well at all, I'm afraid."

"Is it the poison that he got from that beast?" Dave
asked. His brow was furrowed, and he bit his lip. He had
said some rather harsh things about Reb. Perhaps now he
was sorry for them. "He'll be all right, won't he?"

The doctor gave him a steady look before answering.
"Some things we doctors can treat—a broken bone, a
sword cut, an arrow wound, sometimes a fever." Then he
looked down at the pale face of his patient and seemed to
think hard. "There's more to his illness than the poison
from the dragon."

"What do you mean, Doctor?" Jake asked quickly. "I
thought it was just that wound in his arm and the poison
that must have gotten into it."

"That's bad enough, but we've done what we can for
that. What worries me is that there is something else that
I can't exactly put my finger on—he just won't come out of
that coma."

Wash picked up Reb's limp hand and held it tightly. There were tears in his eyes, and he dashed them away with his sleeve. "I should have stayed with him. I shouldn't have let him go out alone."

Josh patted the small boy's shoulder. "Not your fault, Wash," he muttered. "It wouldn't have mattered if all of us had been there. I don't think we could have done a thing."

"What was it that happened?" Abbey asked. Josh knew she never liked sickness and, if she had had her way, would have fled the room. She feared illness, and now alarm was in her eyes. "Did anyone hear what actually happened out there?"

"*We can tell you that.*" Elander entered the room, accompanied by Elaine. He came to the head of the bed where Reb lay, rested his hand on the boy's forehead, then pulled it back. "I knew all the time," he said steadily, "that there was something going on in Reb, but I didn't know what it was exactly. That is, not until Wash told me the story, and then Princess Elaine confirmed it."

"Well, what was it?" Jake demanded. "We couldn't get a word out of Wash." He looked angrily at the boy. "He acted like he was withholding information."

"That's exactly what he *was* doing, Jake." Elendar nodded. "He told me what had happened, and I required him to keep silent. But I can tell you now. Reb encountered one of the most evil beings in the kingdom of the Dark Lord. She calls herself Mogen, and a more foul spirit never set foot on this earth."

"What is she—some kind of a witch?" Jake asked.

"I suppose that is what you would call her. She traffics with evil in every known form. She puts spells on people. She knows of all the worst poisons and herbs, and time and time again I have tried to trap her, but she has avoided me—so far."

Josh looked down at Reb and felt a sudden spasm of fear as he noticed the clamminess of his face.

"He's—he's so sick," Sarah said. "What did she do to him?"

"Well, for one thing, she put this on him." Elendar reached into the pocket of his cloak and pulled forth a metal disk. "This is the amulet of the Dark Lord. You see this strange device carved on it? That is his sign—the bent cross. If you ever see that, you know at once that evil is behind it." His voice was grim, and his eyes flashed. "Anyone who wears it is in danger of his spirit being overwhelmed by the powers that would destroy Camelot. I will destroy the amulet, but I wanted you all to see it so that in your future travels you will be aware of the bent cross."

"Is that what made Reb act so funny?" Wash asked, looking up at the seer.

"Partly that." Elendar nodded. "But it was even worse because, as I said, Mogen knows how to cloud men's minds, and she certainly clouded the mind of our young friend here. I think she touched you too, Wash, but only to put you to sleep so that you would not be aware of her presence. Now some of her power still rests on him."

"The doctors say they don't know what to do." Josh looked over at the doctor, who frowned in reply.

"We just can't do some things," the doctor said.

"Don't blame the physician," Elendar said quickly. "He has done well in binding up the wound and treating the poison from the beast—but it will take more than that. I will do what I can."

The Sleepers watched, and the physician observed even more closely, as Elendar had a bowl brought by a servant. He filled it with water, took a leather pouch out of his cloak, and then removed from it what appeared to be dead leaves. Crumbling them, he let the leaves fall into

151

the water. At once a vapor cloud arose, and a strange odor permeated the room.

"This is the leaf of the carmine tree," he said. "I have found it to be helpful in such cases. Be very still, all of you. You cannot leave the room."

No one tried to leave. They all watched with bated breath. Elendar kept his hands on the head of the sick boy. The fragrance of the carmine leaves rose, a strong odor, and more than once Josh felt his head beginning to swim. *There's something in those leaves,* he said to himself. *I hope it helps Reb!*

All watched Reb's face. He seemed a dead boy. His skin was sallow and clammy, and there was no movement at all for a long time.

Then Josh said, "Look! I saw his eyelids move a little bit!"

At once Elendar called in a loud voice, "Reb, come back! Come back from where you are—and join the house of Goel again."

Everyone seemed to be holding his breath, waiting.

Then Reb's eyelids fluttered.

Sarah gasped and put her fist against her lips. "He's alive! He's alive, and he's not going to die."

As Josh watched Reb's eyelids, they slowly opened.

He seemed confused as he looked around the room, moving his head slightly. Finally he licked his lips, blinked several times, and whispered, "Where—where am I?"

"You are safe, my boy," Elendar said. He took Reb's hands and held them still. "Do not be afraid. You have been on a long and dark journey, but you are back now. How do you feel?"

Reb licked his lips again, cleared his throat, and seemed to gather strength. "Why, I guess I've had a bad dream. Don't know what in the world happened to me." He tried to sit up, and Josh and Dave helped him.

He grinned at them slightly. "Looks like I got a couple of good helpers." He stared down at his bandaged arm, and memory seemed to come back to him. He shut his jaws firmly. "I remember part of it—about that critter that come at me."

Elendar said, "We will pray that most of the memories will fade. But some you should never forget. Do you remember Princess Elaine?"

Reb sat up a little straighter. "Well, I shore do. That big varmint about tore my arm off, and then when I fell back I heard that woman—or whatever she was—screaming, and then I seen you, Princess, shoot an arrow that hit right in the middle of that big snake." He slapped his head and said, "That's about all I remember except he fell over dead, and I guess I must have passed out."

Elendar's eyes were still, and he seemed very relieved. "You are a very fortunate young man, Reb Lee Jackson. Goel has looked out for you well."

"Yep, Goel and the princess here. I ain't never gonna forget that, Princess. I was a gone coon, you bet!"

Something in his voice sounded familiar—a humility and a lightness that had been missing.

"Yes," Elendar said, nodding his silvery head. "He is no longer under the power of Mogen or the Dark Lord. Now he will become himself again."

Elaine said, "I think it might be well if we let him rest some now."

Elendar agreed and bustled about, getting the Sleepers to leave, but Reb called out, "Miss Elaine, you stay just a minute, will you please?"

Elaine hesitated but then, at a nod from Elendar, moved over to stand beside the bed.

When the others had gone, he said, "I don't know how to say this, but I reckon you saved my life."

"It was the doing of Goel," the princess said quickly. She repeated the story of how he had told her that she had been chosen to slay the vicious beast.

Reb listened intently. "You're about the bravest girl I ever saw—to tackle that beast with just one arrow, when knights had failed with all them big spears."

"It was different this time." Elaine smiled. He looked so tired she wanted to reach out and brush his hair back from his forehead where it lay plastered with sweat, but she refrained. "This was at the command of Goel, and the arrow was blessed by him. I knew he never fails."

Watching her, Reb said, "I—I remember some things about what happened, but some things I don't." His jaw tightened, and his face reddened. "I remember one thing, though—I behaved like a stupid mule the last few weeks!"

This time Princess Elaine did brush back the lock of hair. She let her hand rest on his forehead for a moment. "You mustn't torment yourself, Reb. You weren't your-self, as a matter of fact. You are one of the sweetest boys I have ever known. It was that Mogen who made you be-have like you did."

At the mention of Mogen, Reb flushed even more and shut his eyes. "No, I was responsible to do what was right. And I sure made a fool of myself with her, didn't I?"

Elaine drew her hand back and smiled. Then she pushed him down on the bed. "Lie down and sleep now. You'll feel better tomorrow after you've rested."

He looked up. "I don't guess you'd want to go riding with me anymore—not after the way I've acted."

"Of course I'll go riding with you! As soon as you're able. Lie back now and rest. I'll just sit here beside you."

Reb closed his eyes and almost at once was asleep. Elaine arranged the cover around him, sat down, and watched the boy's face for a long time.

* * *

The council sat glumly around the table. Finally Sir Gwin said, "I'm sorry to be the bearer of evil tidings." His face was long, and doubt filled his eyes. "But I felt you should know the worst."

King Dion and Queen Mauve both spoke up at once. "No, you did exactly right, Sir Gwin." King Dion rubbed his chin, then said, "Tell me again about the forces of Melchior. How many do you count in his army?"

"As badly as I hate to say it, Sire, at least three times the number of the men we can muster." Anger leaped into his eyes. "We did not know how effective his trickery was at convincing men."

Sir Elbert's large, round face was gloomy as usual. "There's not much hope, I'm afraid, Your Majesty. We'll do the best we can—but we're surrounded, and we'll have to fight a defensive action."

Sir Nolen stood to the left of Sir Gwin. He was small, but his eyes were gleaming with anger. "We'll never give up, Sire," he burst out suddenly. "If we could get in the clear and fight an action on horseback, I know we could win."

"We can never do that," Sir Gwin said. "Already our scouts have told us that they are closing in on all sides. We had better be prepared to withstand a siege."

"Do we have enough food and water," the queen asked, "to go on for a long time? Once we're surrounded, we cannot break through."

"That is questionable, I'm afraid, Your Majesty," Sir Gwin said. "We will do the best we can and trust the loyal hearts of those knights who have remained with us."

The king looked over at Elendar, who had said nothing but remained in the shadows by the wall. "And what say you, Elendar?"

155

Elendar knew he was being asked for help, for guidance. He stared at the king steadily, then at the queen. Finally he said, "We must walk this road with all the courage we can muster. True, we are outnumbered, but"—he said in a louder voice—"we have right on our side."

Sir Elbert gave him a disappointed look. "Really, Elendar. I was expecting more help than that."

Elendar smiled at the large knight. "You do not trust the right to triumph, Sir Elbert?"

"Well, I don't want to be gloomy about this, but I don't think I can handle more than three of Melchior's knights myself. But we shall see, shall we not?"

"That's the most encouraging thing I ever heard you say." Gwin smiled. "Let us go muster the men."

"How much time do we have before they attack?" the queen asked.

"Not more than a day, I would think," Sir Gwin responded, "and I would ask you, Sire, to stay away from the field of action."

"I will be where the battle is," King Dion said, and his youth seemed to come back to him. His hair was silver now, but his dark blue eyes were clear. He stood, and there was a nobility in him that shone out as he said, "The king will lead the army. If I fall—you, my son, will be the king."

Prince Loren flushed and moved to his father's side. He bowed his head. "I will lay down my life for you, Father, and for Camelot."

The king put his hands on his son's arm. "We must walk closer, my son, for one day you will wear this crown. Come now, let us go inspect the battlements and prepare for the battle."

17

A Bright and Shining Time

Camelot was besieged. Inside, the defenders manned the walls, the women cooked the food, the children carried fresh arrows to the archers who kept their positions high on the wall. But the dark host of Melchior seemed to have brought with them a cloud of despair.

Day after day went by, and every moment was critical. By day, Melchior's archers sometimes launched such a flight of black arrows that they seemed to darken the sun. By night, they shot flaming torches so that the defenders were hard put to keep the fires extinguished.

Throughout all the days of battle the Seven Sleepers were busy. The girls helped with the cooking and cared for the wounded until their eyes grew gritty from lack of sleep and their nerves raw from the moans of the wounded men they treated.

One morning Sarah paused and looked over at Abigail, whose face was smudged with dirt. Sarah smiled. "Do you know—this is the first time I've ever seen you get dirty. You're usually neat as a pin."

Abbey had been bathing the face of a young soldier who had taken an arrow in the side. He was in a high fever, and, as she tended him, for once in her life she seemed to have forgotten her own vanity.

Abbey looked down at her dirty clothing—which had not been washed for she knew not how long—and at her broken nails. Then she reached up and touched her face. "I'm a mess," she said. "But I guess this is no time to be fixing our hair or polishing our nails, is it, Sarah?"

Sarah put her arm around the younger girl. She had always been jealous of Abigail's beauty and critical of her selfishness, but now, despite her fatigue, she was warmed by the girl's efforts. "You've done a beautiful job, Abbey. I know everyone has noticed how hard you've worked."

Abigail flushed. She was used to compliments, but always these were on her beauty and not on her qualities of diligence, of which she was well aware she had little. "How long do you think we can hold out?" she asked, changing the subject.

As if in answer to her question, Josh came by, looked at the wounded man, and frowned. "I wish he hadn't been wounded. We're so thin in the ranks now that I don't see how we can possibly hold out much longer."

The two girls looked at one another with concern, but it was Sarah who ventured to ask, "Is it that bad, Josh?"

Josh took out a handkerchief, wiped his forehead, then replaced it. "It's about as dark as it can get, I guess. I thought Sir Elbert was the most pessimistic man I ever saw, but he's downright cheerful compared to some of the other fellows. I don't see how we can go on much longer."

At that moment, a cry was heard. "To the wall—to the south wall!"

Without a word, Josh turned and ran.

The girls stared at each other and then followed. They watched Josh scramble up a ladder to stand on the boards that held the archers. They saw him pick up a bow and send arrow after arrow downward.

Then Elendar came by and snapped, "You girls— take cover!"

As if to emphasize his words, a steel-tipped arrow sailed over the wall and struck a timber not six inches from Sarah's head. It quivered there, and she looked at it in shock. "Come on, Abbey. Let's get out of this. We can't do any good if we get pinned to the wall with one of those arrows."

* * *

Elendar ran to the wall. He was like the others—dirty and battle-worn. Time after time it had been Elendar who rallied the defenders. Now he climbed the ladder one more time.

Just as he reached the top, a steel-tipped helmet with a black plume appeared above the wall. Without thought Elendar seized a battle-ax leaning against the parapet and, just as the man prepared to vault over, brought it down with such force that it split the metal helmet in two. The man went tumbling down.

A cry went up from the onlookers. "Elendar! Elendar!"

Then, as the valiant seer began cleaving right and left, the other men gave themselves to the battle. It was a perilous time, for they had to conserve their arrows. They were reduced now to using those that came at them over the walls, and each man waited until he was sure of his shot.

But finally the attack was beaten off, and the soldiers of Melchior retreated back out of range of the archers.

Elendar looked down at his hand—it had been gashed across the back—pulled out a handkerchief, and wrapped it.

Josh came up beside him. "You'd better have that looked at. I think they are using poison on some of these arrows."

"I will when I have time." Elendar was short-spoken, for he alone knew how serious the matter was. He walked away and went to where the king and Prince Loren were panting as they stared down at the retreating enemy.

King Dion looked around, and his face was lined and worn. "It was a close thing, eh?"

"Yes, Your Majesty, and they'll be back."

Prince Loren lifted his eyes to the seer and said firmly, "We can last. I think we ought to make a surprise attack. Catch them when they're not looking."

Elendar looked at the boy fondly. "A charge, you mean?"

"Yes. I'll lead it," the prince said recklessly.

King Dion looked at his tall son proudly. "You would too, wouldn't you, Loren? I'm glad to see that you have such courage. But I think we must wait before we try a thing like that. It can only work once, and we have to catch them completely off guard."

"You haven't lost your sense of tactics, Your Majesty." Elendar nodded with approval. "Our time will come."

Loren bit his lip, then abruptly changed the subject. "What's the matter with Sir Reb?" he demanded suddenly. "He's not too badly wounded to fight, is he? We need him."

Elendar did not answer at once. Then he said, "The wounds that the young man took in the flesh are healed." He caught King Dion's eye. "The wounds of the spirit are harder, but I pray that he will be completely healed soon."

King Dion wagged his head. "What a sad thing. He did such mighty things, and now he feels it was all wasted. I wish the boy could get better."

"So do I." Elendar nodded shortly. Then he walked away, muttering under his breath, "None of them know how deep the wounds of the darkness go when they enter a man's spirit. It's only a miracle that the boy is alive, after all he went through!"

Elendar wanted to go to Sir Reb—and he had gone many times—but now he knew that he had done all he could. Besides, he had his hands full with the battle that would soon be raging again. But as he went to his cot to take a little rest, he said aloud, "Goel, that young man needs something that I can't give him—something that only you can give."

* * *

Reb sat in his chamber staring at the door. He had done this for hours, and even now he felt a fear that he could not explain. He looked down at his arm and saw that the jagged wound was knitted together. The scar would always be visible, but physically he knew that he was healed.

"What's the matter with me?" He groaned. "Here I sit in this dumb room, while outside my friends and the king and all the knights are fighting for their lives! And I can't even go through that door."

He got to his feet, picked up his sword, and marched toward the entrance. But the closer he got, the more his steps dragged. Fear rose in him like a dark tide, and when he was five feet away from the door it became so great that he felt as if a pair of steely hands had seized him by the throat. With a cry of despair, he dropped his sword, moved back from the door, and slumped in a chair, his face in his hands.

How long he sat there he never knew. He thought of the dark time when he had fallen under the power of Mogen. He thought of the time since, when he had healed physically but had not been able to shake off fear. He was a tough young man, Bob Lee Jackson, but he did not feel tough now, and he felt the tears gather in his eyes as he realized how he had failed his friends.

The door creaked slightly, and Reb looked up, then jumped to his feet. "Elaine," he said shortly. He wanted to say more, but he felt such shame for what he had become that he could not speak.

Elaine came in, and he saw that her eyes were weary and that her clothing was dirty and dingy. But her voice was soft as she said, "I came to see if you were all right, Reb."

"You mean," he said sharply, "you came to see if I'm still a coward."

"No—"

"That's what everybody's saying—that I'm a coward!" Reb burst out. He slapped one fist in his palm. "And you know, they're right! I *am* a coward. Elaine, I'm afraid even to go out that door."

"I know," she said, her eyes filled with compassion. "Elendar has told me why that is. You're still struggling with the spell that Mogen put on you."

"No, I'm just a blamed coward, and that's all there is to it." Reb walked away, unable to face her. Leaning with his face against the wall, he muttered, "Don't stay here with me. Go out there with those who have some insides to 'em."

Quietly she said, "Reb, Goel does nothing foolishly. Nothing he does is wasted. If he saved your life, he saved it for a purpose." She hesitated, then added, "I know that you'll once again be the Reb that I knew." Then she turned and left the room.

When the door shut, Reb looked up wildly. His eyes were filled with doubt and confusion, and he slumped down again, put his forehead in his hands, despair written in every line of his body. He never knew how long he stayed like that, thinking of the past, regretting all that had gone before, remembering the things that he had done that were wrong, the pride that had been in him.

"Reb, you must not think of yourself in such a way."

Reb leaped to his feet and turned.

"Goel!"

The tall, familiar figure stood before him.

Reb took a step forward, but then remembered what he had done, and shame filled him. He wanted to run, flee the gray eyes that watched him so carefully, but he could only swallow and stand there waiting.

"It is a good thing for a young man to learn his weakness. He will remember and avoid it in the future," Goel said. "I warned you once, my boy, that you had too much pride—that it would have to be broken before you would be the young man I want you to be."

"I remember," Reb broke in, his voice hoarse. "Why didn't I listen to you?"

"You are young, and this has been a hard lesson." Goel watched as the young man's head suddenly dropped, and without hesitation Goel put his arm around his shaking shoulders. "Never be ashamed of honest tears. Any man or any woman who can't weep over wrongs they have done—why, they're not complete."

Goel held the boy within his strong grasp, then he stepped in front of Reb and took him by his shoulders. When the young man's head came up, he said with a smile, "Now, that's in the past. We need not speak of it any longer."

But Reb cried, "I can't even go through that door!"

"That was because of your weakness. You were alone in here, and you felt that, did you not?"

"I never felt so lonesome in all my life," Reb cried earnestly.

"Let me tell you one thing, and then I must leave. There is such a thing as a person being alone—but there is such a thing as an Inner Presence. That is what I want you to learn, my boy. In a few moments you will not see me any longer—with your eyes, that is. But I want you to promise me that you will believe that I am somehow within you. Can you believe that?"

Reb looked into the eyes of Goel. "If you say it, Goel, then I'll believe it, whether I feel it or not."

"That's my Reb." Goel clapped the boy's shoulder heartily. He laughed, and there was a freedom in him that communicated itself to Reb. "Put your sword on. Go help your brethren who are at war," he said.

Reb whirled and ran across the room, seized his sword belt, buckled it, took up his fallen sword, and said, "Yes, I'll go—" and then he discovered that he was alone. "Well, what ever—" He stared around the room wildly and then remembered what Goel had said.

"All right, I'm going through that door, Goel—me and you!" He still felt fear, but with a cry he rushed out shouting, *"For Goel!"*

* * *

Reb and Josh perched on a parapet of the wall, and there seemed to be little enemy activity below.

Josh looked over fondly. "Reb, I think you ought to take a nap or something. You've been on your feet ever since you came back two days ago. You've got to sleep sometime."

Reb had on his tall cowboy hat. He had laid aside his helmet and replaced it with the Stetson. Now, from underneath the brim, his warm, bright blue eyes glinted. "I guess I lost enough time when I was fooling around in that room. Got to make up for it, Josh."

Though Josh seemed glad to see Reb back, his old self again, he had said only, "It's good to have you back, Reb, in every way." But now he said, "I wish there were a thousand Rebels like you. We'd take 'em all."

Reb had been thinking hard about the siege. "You know, Josh. I got me an idea. Have you noticed the last two times they've charged out of that grove of trees? I think they know this side of the wall's the weakest. I'm gambling they're gonna try it again, almost any time."

Josh looked over the wall and saw the gleam of armor under the cover of trees. "I believe you're right. We'd better get some help around here to stand them off."

Reb shook his head. "We can't do it forever. I say we got to do something different."

"Different? Like what?"

"Like Stonewall Jackson did at Second Manassas. He let the Yankees go right by and when they were through, he hit 'em in the rear. Whipped the daylights out of 'em—that time, anyway."

Josh thought about that, then nodded slowly. "It might work, but I doubt if the king would let us try it."

"Let's find out," Reb said.

Ten minutes later Josh and Reb stood before Elendar and the king and Prince Loren. Reb laid out his plan quickly.

Elendar nodded. "I see what you mean. I noticed the same thing—they always attack that part of the wall."

"That's right," Reb said excitedly, "and what I say we should do is sneak some men out the other side, let them work their way around, and when Melchior's men hit those ladders, we hit *them* from the rear. They won't have no place to retreat to. That kinda discourages a fellow a little bit."

Loren brightened. "I think Reb's right. Father, let's try it."

Dion looked at the two young men. "So be it. You two take the flanks. Reb, you work your way around to the east. Loren, to the west. When they charge, let them get up on the ladders, then hit them with everything you have."

Reb wanted to let out a Rebel yell, but he said, "That's business, Your Majesty! Come on, Loren."

Within thirty minutes the two forces had crept out the back of Camelot, having arranged a trumpet blast sig-

165

nal. "When you hear that," Reb said, "you hit 'em, and I'll hit 'em, and we'll scrunch them critters!"

Reb led his men around the wall, keeping out of sight behind the grove of trees that shielded the castle. Josh and Dave, Wash and Jake—all were with him.

Reb said, "Now, when we hit, hit with everything you've got, all right?"

Suddenly he heard Melchior's men shout as they charged the castle walls. "Let 'em get up them ladders," he whispered, "then we got 'em."

He watched carefully and when all the dark-clad knights had emerged from the woods and were scrambling up the ladders, he took the horn that was secured around his neck by a lanyard and blew with all his might. "Come on!" he shouted. "Get 'em!"

There followed a wild melee. Loren's small force struck the enemy on one flank while Reb's force struck them on the other. Melchior's men looked back and saw that their retreat was cut off. Screaming with rage and fear, they scrambled down the ladders only to meet the sword points of the forces that had trapped them.

"We got 'em! We got 'em!" Reb yelled.

But at that moment, a tall form suddenly appeared in front of him. It was Melchior himself.

"I'll cut that lad down," he shouted to his lieutenant, "and the rest will run."

Reb barely had time to get his sword up to block the blow that Melchior sent downward. There was a clash of metal, and sparks, and Reb was driven back. Then he scrambled to his feet just in time to keep Melchior's sword from striking right at the top of his Stetson.

The blow struck the ground instead, and instantly Reb took his sword with both hands like a baseball bat, swung it mightily, and caught Melchior in the front of the helmet.

The impact drove the helmet back, and Melchior uttered a short cry. He fell backward to the ground. And before he could move, Reb jerked off the dark knight's helmet, and the rest of the Sleepers put the points of their swords to his throat.

"Don't . . . don't kill me," Melchior begged. "I surrender."

It took but a few minutes for the forces of Melchior to see that their leader was defeated. Everywhere the cry of victory went up from the defenders of Camelot and cries of defeat from the dark-clad knights.

And it was not long before King Dion stood before his begrimed, bloody warriors. "You've all been knights of the realm. Your honor and courage will remain forever—and will be sung by minstrels throughout my kingdom. Especially to you" —he turned to the small group at his side— "the Seven Sleepers, we owe a debt of gratitude. How can we ever repay you?"

Smiling, Josh nudged Reb and whispered, "Say something, you bonklehead!"

Reb swallowed and lifted his hat, put it over his heart. "I pledge allegiance—no, that was back in Oldworld. But I'll say this, we ain't never seen nobody like you folks, and we're proud to be a part." He thought for one moment and added, "If I couldn't serve under General Stonewall Jackson, King Dion, I guess I'd choose to serve under you and your folks here!"

18
Good-bye to Camelot

The celebration that took place after the victory of the servants of Goel was forever recorded in the annals of Camelot as the greatest that ever took place in that court.

The royal cooks outdid themselves. When the feast day came, the tables were piled high with joints of mutton, venison, pork, fish, chicken, and every other sort of meat that could be procured. Musicians came from all over the kingdom and played with all their might. Dancers performed with agility and glee before the king and queen and prince and princess.

To the royal family's right, at a special table, the Seven Sleepers were arrayed. Each wore around his neck a gold chain and medallion with the seal of Camelot—gifts of the king. Speeches were made and their virtues praised until Wash said, "Is that us they're talking about? I didn't know we was such cool cats!"

Reb, sitting next to Wash, said, "That reminds me of a woman who lost her husband, back in Arkansas. At the funeral the preacher started going on about what a fine man he was, how wonderful he was, all the good things he had done, and the widow, she leaned over and said to the oldest boy, 'Henry, go up and be shore that's yore pa in that there coffin!'"

Wash laughed out loud, and Josh demanded to know what was so funny.

"Nothing much, Josh," Reb said. "Me and Wash are just glad there ain't no more dragons to kill or battles to fight." He looked about the table. "I do wish there was some good old grits here though."

Dave grinned at him broadly. "I expect they'd get it for us if they knew what it was."

Jake was talking with Abigail and Sarah, explaining how, if they would let *him* run the kingdom, he'd put it on a democratic basis, and then they'd have to elect the king.

"I don't think Prince Loren would like that," Abbey said with a smile. "He thinks he ought to be king because he's King Dion's son."

"That's a pretty bad system," Jake protested. "Everybody ought to have an equal chance at being king."

Sarah laughed. "The democratic system works pretty badly sometimes too. Though mostly it's better than any of the rest," she added.

At that moment, a trumpet blew. Everybody stood, for the king and queen had risen.

"A toast," the king said, "to the valiant Seven Sleepers, Goel's gift to the Kingdom of Camelot."

All around, golden and silver goblets were raised while the health of the seven was drunk. Then King Dion said loudly, "I do proclaim the Seven Sleepers citizens forever of the realm of Camelot. May their lives be prosperous. May they always be as true to one another as they have been to me and my kingdom!"

It was Josh who, at the insistence of the others, answered the toast. "Your Majesty, lords, ladies," he said, "I give you King Dion, Queen Mauve, Princess Elaine, and Prince Loren. I give you the Royal Knights of the Table of Camelot. I give you the good people of Camelot." He held his cup high, and said, "Never have I found hearts so true as I have found in this place. To Camelot—may it always be as it is now."

* * *

170

Afterward, the Sleepers walked back to their quarters.

Sarah took Josh's arm. "You're getting to be quite eloquent, Josh." She looked up at him. "And taller too."

"You just like me because I'm tall," he said. "That's the only reason."

Sarah laughed. "No, there are other reasons than that."

"Like what?"

"I won't tell you. You'd get too vain."

The two passed on down the way, and the others followed, going to their rooms for the night.

Reb stopped to pass a word with Sir Gwin, so he left later than the others. On his way out of the banqueting room, he was met by the Princess Elaine.

She looked very beautiful in her royal blue gown with her hair done up and held in place by silver pins. She lifted her face to his. "Will we ever go for rides again?"

"Tomorrow," Reb promised eagerly. "At sunrise."

"I'll meet you at the gate."

Reb went to his quarters, opened the door, and discovered that the other Sleepers were all inside. He looked wildly around and then saw Goel standing to one side. His mouth dropped open.

Wash joggled his arm. "Shut your mouth, Reb. A bird might fly in there."

Reb clamped his teeth together. "What's happening?"

Josh smiled at him. "What always happens, Reb. As soon as we finish one quest, we're off on another."

Goel seemed to see the look of disappointment on Reb's face. "Aren't you ready to leave, Reb? After all, my work is done here."

Reb wanted to say, "Not right away," but, feeling the eyes of the others, he could do nothing else than nod his head. "Yes, Goel. I'll go anywhere you please."

"Get your things together—we leave at once," Goel commanded.

An hour later they were mounted and moving through the woods.

Reb looked back at the towers of Camelot, and sadness came over him.

Wash said, "You'd like to stay a while, wouldn't you, Reb?"

"Well, just for a little while. You know—" He stopped, unable to explain himself. He said nothing more, and finally he found himself riding alone in the rear.

The night sounds came, an owl called far overhead, and he was startled when the voice of Goel sounded beside him. "You like it at Camelot, don't you, Reb?"

"Yes, I shore do! I like it better than any place I've ever been." Reb looked back, and, although the castle had faded, he could still see in his mind the plumes on the crests of the knights' helmets, the pennants that fluttered gaily in the breeze at the joust, the hawks that flew from the wrists of the hawkers. He looked across at Goel in the moonlight. "Goel, it just seems like I belong in a place like this."

The moonlight was reflected in Goel's eyes, and Reb saw that he was smiling.

"Don't be afraid of the future, Sir Reb," Goel said. "I have the feeling that one day, when the world is rid of the Dark Power, you will be back in Camelot."

Reb sat up straight in the saddle, and a thrill of pure joy ran through him. "If you say so, Goel," he said, "then it's got to be."

The procession passed on down the trail, and darkness closed in upon the woods. All Seven Sleepers were thinking of Camelot, of the king and queen, the prince and princess, the friends they had made, but they were also all wondering the same thing: "Where will Goel send us now?"

Get swept away in the many Gilbert Morris adventures from Moody

Kerrigan Kids #1

The Kerrigan Kids are headed to Africa to take pictures and write a story on a once fierce tribe. The Kids may be able to travel to Africa but if Duffy can't learn to swallow her pride and appreciate others, they may be left behind with their dreaded Aunt Minnie!
ISBN#0-8024-1578-4

Kerrigan Kids #2

With a whole countryful of places to explore and exciting new adventures to be had, the Kerrigan Kids can't help but have a good time in England. The Kerrigan Kids also learn an important lesson about having a good attitude and about being a good friend.
ISBN#0-8024-1579-2

Kerrigan Kids #3

After several mishaps including misdirected luggage, the Kerrigans are reminded that bad things can happen to good people and the importance of trusting in God even during difficult circumstances.
ISBN#0-8024-1580-6

Kerrigan Kids #4

The Sunday before they leave, the kids are reminded of the story of the Good Samaritan. When there is no one to meet their two new friends from the plane trip at the airport, the Kerrigan clan puts what they learned about helping other into practice.
ISBN#0-8024-1580-6

Get swept away in the many Gilbert
Morris Adventures from Moody Press:

"Too Smart" Jones Series

Join Juliet "Too Smart" Jones and
her homeschooled friends as they
attempt to solve exciting myster-
ies. Active Series for ages 7-12.

**Dixie Morris Animal
Adventures**

Follow the exciting adventures of
this animal lover as she learns
more of God and His character
through her many adventures
underneath the Big Top. Ten Book
Series for ages 7-12.

The Daystar Voyages

Join the crew of the Daystar as they
traverse the wide expanse of space.
Adventure and danger abound, but
they learn time and again that God is
truly the Master of the Universe.
Active Series for ages 10-14.

Bonnets and Bugles Series

Follow good friends Leah Carter and Jeff
Majors as they experience danger, intrigue,
compassion, and love in these civil war
adventures. Ten Book Series for ages 10-14.

The Seven Sleepers Series

Go with Josh and his friends as they are sent
by Goel, their spiritual leader, on dangerous
and challenging voyages to conquer the forces
of darkness in the new world. Ten Book
Series for ages 10-14. Watch for the new Lost
Chronicles of the Seven Sleepers!